Rowan's Renewal

Kinks & Conundrums Book 2

Anna Sparrows

Acknowledgements

For Erin.
Thank you for encouraging me to step outside my comfort zone and try something new.

Acknowledgements

Rowan's Renewal is a **sweet**, summer vacation themed novella which features hurt/comfort themes, a Younger Daddy/Older Boy kink dynamic, a first time Boy, and ABDL themes (without much of the AB).

That said, this book does contain **self-deprecation, embarrassment** and **self-esteem issues, incontinence, erectile dysfunction**, and **watersports** and other elements suited to readers over the age of 18.

I am still a firm believer in not yucking someone else's yum, so if the above isn't for you, don't force yourself to read it.

Life's too short to read something you don't enjoy.

Acknowledgements

Firstly, thank you to Anna, Jamie Lee, and Marianne at the *Daddy Kink and Age Gap MM books group* on Facebook. This book is originally being published as part of the *DKAG Summer Shorts* novella series, in celebration of the Facebook group — a place which always makes me happy. Thank you for including me in this series, and for all your support over the years.

Secondly, thanks to my wonderful alpha readers, Cassidy Lane and Erin Nelson. Your encouragement and feedback made this a very enjoyable write for me.

Thank you as well to my amazing PA, Ky, for pushing me when necessary, and for designing the *Kinks & Conundrums* cover. Similarly, thank you to Joe Satoria for the *DKAG Summer Shorts* ebook cover!

Finally, thank you for reading and for giving my books a chance. I really hope you enjoy it!

Contents

Chapter One

"**W**hat. The. Fuck?"

Probably not the most grateful way to accept a birthday present, but there are no other words right now. The piece of paper in front of me has got to be a joke, right?

Across the table from me, my former best friend grins widely. "You're going to *love it*," she says, blowing her dark bangs out of her eyes a second later. "And a vacation is *exactly* what you need to get over the whole Alex fiasco."

The whole Alex fiasco. Better known as four years of my life wasted on a selfish prick of a man. A selfish prick of a man I'd settled for because I didn't think anyone else would want me.

Alex didn't even want me in the end.

Nevertheless, the kind of vacation which would relax me is *not* the kind of vacation my best friend has so lovingly booked to celebrate my forty-first birthday.

"Bianca," I begin slowly, "in the twenty-something years you've known me, have I ever once given any indication that I like" —I take a quick glance at the brochure that came with the ticket— "sun, sand, and *short-shorts*?"

She rolls her eyes. "*Everyone* loves those things."

"Not me." Dropping the papers back onto the tabletop between us, I fold my arms and sigh. "I *hate* the heat. I barely passed swim class at school. And I *never* wear shorts." Especially the kind that reveal way too much about a person or their underwear of choice.

"Oh, stop being such a grouch," she waves dismissively, then leans forward for a sip of her mimosa. "When was the last time you went to a beach? Or took any kind of vacation at all?" Another sip. I can almost taste the fizz on my own tongue. "Even the Editor-In-Chief of a world famous—"

"Hardly."

"—*world famous* lifestyle magazine needs some downtime every now and then."

"Fine. A vacation would be nice." Especially after the Alex fiasco. And great, now I'm saying it. I sigh. "But I don't like the heat. Or sand. Or wearing shorts."

"Too bad," Bianca flits her bright pink manicure at the ticket and brochure on the table, "because that trip is non-refundable." Her lips curl upwards wickedly. "It's a gay resort, Rowan. You can enjoy watching other men wearing shorts. Relax under an umbrella with a fruity cocktail and just let go for a week." She gestures outside, where people are rugged up in thick winter coats and puffy jackets, battling the chill of January. It doesn't snow here, but the winds are icy and brittle. "You really prefer this?"

I do, actually. At least, I prefer being able to wear big, puffy jackets and long coats. Bulky sweatpants or thick denim. Long sweaters.

Clothes that cover my shameful secret.

A secret that Bianca, as much as I adore her, knows nothing about.

"I like the cold," I insist. "I know that makes me weird, but I prefer cuddling up in front of a fireplace with a glass of merlot and a good book to risking skin cancer and getting sand in places sand really doesn't belong."

"This trip might change your mind."

"Also," I scowl at her, jabbing my index finger at the brochure, "this resort is in Australia! You want me to fly for over, what, fourteen hours just to sit on a beach somewhere? Why couldn't you have picked somewhere closer? Like...Mexico. Or Hawaii." I'm not sure what the weather at either destination is like this time of year, but I can't imagine any resort is worth a fourteen-hour flight.

The very idea of being stuck on a plane for that long makes me feel sick.

What if someone notices...?

No. Nope. Nuh-uh. I am not going, and that is final.

Famous last words.

Chapter Two

Aaron

"So, how is it you managed to score yourself some vacation time when you only just started working here?" my colleague, Vince, teases good naturedly as we walk down a brightly lit hallway together.

Our shoes squeak on the linoleum floors, but they're not really audible over the rest of the hustle and bustle around us. Machines beeping, low, murmured conversations, children crying, and occasionally someone calling out for assistance set the backdrop of the emergency department where we work.

"My leave was approved before I transferred," I shrug. "I've been hanging out for this trip for a long-ass time, man."

I originally booked it with my boyfriend. Well, you know, before he told me he'd fallen out of love with me and thought we'd be better off as friends. *That* had led to me packing my bags and leaving the apartment we'd shared, and requesting a transfer to a sister hospital, not really wanting to work with my ex anymore.

Because I booked the trip, I got to keep the tickets. Three weeks in Australia, culminating in one week at a 'clothing optional, adults only, LGBTQ+ beach resort' (per the brochure) sounded like the perfect way to get over my heartbreak.

I mean, isn't that what people say now? That the best way to get over someone is to get under someone new?

I'm vers, so I'll get on top, or under, or go sideways...I really don't have a preference. As long as it isn't with Jerry.

"And you're going by yourself?" Vince asks, arching a dark eyebrow. He's a big, gorgeous bear of a man, complete with a cuddly belly. But it's his personality —always so concerned for everyone else— that really makes him attractive.

It's a pity he's taken. I would have offered for him to come with me, otherwise.

Get it? *Come* with me?

Dear God, I need to get laid.

"I am," I nod, grinning. "I love the idea of getting to explore by myself. I set the itinerary. I get to decide if the souvenirs I'm buying are too tacky. Just me."

"I feel like there's a story there," Vince chuckles as we reach the triage station and reach for our respective clipboards.

"Jerry was an asshole," I tell him, already flipping through the notes for my first case of the night, "that's the whole story."

He snorts. "That will win you a Pulitzer."

I raise my middle finger with a laugh as we head in opposite directions.

Transferring jobs and moving halfway across the country following my breakup was a pain in the ass, but I'm making friends and settling in well...and I leave on vacation tomorrow, which is the cherry on top!

***

The first two weeks of my adventure seem to evaporate in the heat of the Australian sun. I have made my way up the eastern coast, visiting Melbourne, then Sydney, then the Gold Coast and Brisbane, but the final week has been reserved for the pièce de résistance: an LGBTQ+ Adults Only beachfront resort on the Sunshine Coast.

The promotional materials are what really drew me in. With its own private clothing-optional beach, a huge pool, brightly colored décor, and modern, recently renovated suites, the resort sounded like heaven. After two weeks of non-stop exploration and travel, drinking cocktails and relaxing at a resort before I have to fly home is exactly what the doctor ordered.

(It's me — I'm the doctor.)

When my Uber pulls to a stop outside the resort, nestled as it is in what seems to be its own tropical rainforest, I take a moment to smile up at the welcoming main building. Painted white, the front doors are bi-folding, opened all the way to entice in the sea-breeze as well as guests. From the curb, I can see the large wooden fan suspending from the vaulted ceilings, and the white floor tiles gleam enticingly, too. It looks like a big, airy space filled with natural light — perfect for a coastal retreat like this one.

Climbing the five or so front stairs to enter the sprawling foyer, I feel instantly relaxed by how open and bright it is. They've brought the outside in as well, with large, leafy potted plants dotted around the space, really playing off the 'rainforest meets beach' aesthetic.

I already want to live here and never leave. Sadly, I'm only here for six nights before I have to fly back home.

Rolling my suitcase across the tiles towards the reception desk, I can't help but check out the attractive man leaning over the distressed timber counter, talking quietly with the concierge. The first thing I notice about him is his thick, dark brown hair and the few silvery streaks glinting in the early afternoon sunlight. The next is his sharp, square jawline, emphasized by salt and pepper stubble. Then my gaze travels over his strong shoulders and back, clothed as it is by a pale blue polo shirt. Sadly, his probably perfect ass is hidden behind the waffle knit sweater wrapped around his waist, over the top of baggy beige cargo pants.

The poor guy has to be sweltering in an outfit like that. Even the polo shirt material looks too thick and non-breathable for the humidity here.

Sure enough, as I get closer, I can see the sheen of sweat on his pale forehead and under his pretty blue eyes, which seem bright against the contrast of the dark bags under them.

"...apologize, Mister Stratton," the concierge says apologetically, their nose scrunching as they type frantically at their keyboard. "I don't know how this could have happened. The system is supposed to prevent double bookings."

The guy's shoulders slump, and he hangs his head. There's something almost heartbreaking in the expression on his face; like resignation and fear combined. He shifts uncomfortably on his feet, and his (surprisingly American) voice is thick as he asks, "Where am I supposed to go?"

If his expression had been heartbreaking, the plaintive question is like a sucker punch.

Even the concierge's face crumples.

"I've booked a two-bedroom suite," the words leave my mouth before I can think the offer through. "I'm here for six nights. Would you like my second room for a few days? The whole time?"

The guy turns around to face me and he's even more attractive front-on. With a perfectly straight nose dusted with freckles, bright blue (though tired) eyes, and full lips, it takes me more than a few seconds to comprehend the fact that he is speaking.

"—dn't possibly…"

"Please," I insist, offering him what I hope is a charming smile. "I, uh, originally booked this trip with my boyfriend and…" I trail off, not thinking it necessary to explain *why* we had wanted a second bedroom on hand. "Well, we broke up and plans changed. I was going to see if I could downgrade to a single or a studio, but I'm guessing that's not an option."

"We're booked solid, I'm afraid," the concierge nods. Then they turn back to the stranger I've just invited to share my room. "We will refund your booking immediately. And, should you take Mister…?"

"Park," I supply helpfully, "Aaron Park."

They type away on their keyboard again, smiling softly. "If you should take Mister Park up on his offer, I will make sure the booking is upgraded to include complimentary hire of all motorized and non-motorized watersports equipment and daily breakfast for you both."

The stranger chews his bottom lip and squirms for a moment. There's a flash of something undefinable over his face before he swallows and nods. "If you're sure it won't be a problem…"

"I can't see why it would be. I wasn't going to use the second room, so I'm glad it isn't going to waste."

He shuffles on his feet, a blush dusting his cheeks as he averts his gaze. "Thank you. I…" he clears his throat. "Thanks. I, um, I'm staying the six nights, too. Then flying back home after that."

I smile. "Home as in America, or…?"

"Oh, yeah. America." He grimaces. "I'm not looking forward to that return flight. The one to get here was bad enough."

To punctuate the sentiment, he reaches for his large, black, hard-shelled rolling suitcase, his fingers flexing over the handle.

"Anyway," the concierge interrupts, "I've got you both checked in to room four-oh-seven." They lean forward and hand us each a room key before running through the layout of the resort, detailing the pool and jacuzzi hours, where to hire kayaks, jet skis and snorkeling gear, and what time the on-site restaurant serves its buffet breakfast.

My roommate for the week seems to become increasingly fidgety the longer the concierge speaks. He all but heaves a sigh of relief when we're finally directed towards the elevator, seemingly in a rush to get to the room.

Away from the desk, it feels a little more awkward to be heading towards a hotel room I will be sharing with a complete stranger, but I don't regret my offer. Even though the second bedroom won't be used as the playroom-slash-nursery away from home Jerry and I had planned on, I am glad someone is going to make use of it. Especially when the sweet stranger seemed almost on the verge of tears with the booking snafu.

I've always been a sucker for a sweet Boy in need of a rescue, I guess. That's the Daddy in me, and it's been too long since I last let him out to play.

Maybe when I get back home, I'll visit the local kink club I've heard about. I've hooked up a couple of times on this holiday, and it has been great, but my need to nurture and connect on a deeper level clearly needs to be satisfied just as badly.

"So, roomie," I joke to ease some of the awkwardness as we wait for the elevator, "I'm Aaron."

His shoulders are tense, but the sheepish smile on his face is adorable. "Shit. Sorry. I didn't think to introduce myself. I'm

Rowan. Rowan Stratton." He extends the hand not gripping his suitcase like a lifeline and I shake it. He shifts uncomfortably and cringes a little. "Thanks again for the rescue."

"Seriously," I laugh just as the elevator doors swing open and a gaggle of cute, giggly twinks spill out, brushing past us as they talk loudly in broad Australian accents about finding the bar, "you don't have to thank me. I'm just glad you didn't think I'm some weirdo freak for offering."

"I'll be honest," he leans against the mirrored wall of the elevator, full lips drawing into a tiny smirk, "I'm half expecting you to harvest my organs or something. Hot young guys aren't usually lining up at my door, you know?"

"I'm thirty-two, hardly a spring chicken," I chuckle. "But I *am* a doctor, so the organ harvesting *is* a plausible side-hustle..."

"Thirty-two seems forever ago for me," his tone is wistful, and his smile is soft. Then his lips quirk into something a little rueful and wry. "I just turned forty-one. So, yeah, you're young."

The elevator lets us off on the fourth floor and we make our way to room seven. Rowan swipes his key and pushes the door open, throwing a hasty apology over his shoulder as he bustles forward and starts glancing into doorways.

With an exhaled "Oh, thank God," he pushes into one of the rooms, dragging his suitcase with him, shutting and locking the door behind him with an audible click.

After my own quick perusal of the apartment, I realize he must be in the bathroom.

I guess that's what all the fidgeting was about.

I want to smack myself upside the head. I've seen enough potty dances in my time, after all. Both as a doctor *and* as an age play Daddy.

I guess I wasn't completely projecting after all.

Chapter Three

Aaron Park has got to be a figment of my imagination. Some fantasy creation from the deep, dark recesses of my brain. Because there's no way a man like him is real. Maybe I finally had some kind of breakdown when the nice concierge told me about the system double booking my room, and everything since that moment has been a hallucination.

Except, no. If I was fantasizing, I definitely wouldn't be changing a sodden pair of incontinence pants while my super hot young rescuer lurks somewhere in the apartment beyond the closed bathroom door.

If I were fantasizing, fantasy-me wouldn't have been diagnosed with a rare case of prostate cancer in my late teens, and fantasy-me *certainly* wouldn't have endured complications from the surgery which left me without a prostate and with permanent incontinence.

So *Doctor* Aaron Park —because of *course* he's also a doctor!— can't actually be a product of my hysterical imaginings.

With thick, jet-black hair, dark soulful eyes, and flawless gold-toned skin, he's handsome, funny, and a good Samaritan. Sure, he's a lot younger than any of the men I've dated (not that I've dated many, considering my condition), but I can't help finding him attractive.

Being alone for the better part of a year isn't helping my attraction to him, either. Plus, it's a fatal flaw of mine to be attracted to any scrap of kindness. I know that's not the healthiest way to be, either, but this is what happens every time a guy is even remotely nice to me.

I start forming attachments.

I *can't* get attached to Dr. Aaron Park. Firstly, because we've only known each other for, like, five minutes, so that's just weird. Secondly, because I don't know anything about him, aside from the fact that he says he's a doctor and he also lives somewhere in America. Thirdly, because I have no idea *where* he lives back home, and we are only staying here for a week.

But finally, and most importantly, he's too young to be saddled with a permanently incontinent old man for any amount of time. Not even for this week.

Not for the first time in my life, or even in the past twenty-four hours, I wish my situation was wildly different. The flight here was every part as awful as I thought it would be, with me choosing to practically live in the plane's bathrooms (to the point where I think the woman stuck in the seat beside me was afraid I had some kind of stomach bug). Thankfully, entering the country through Customs was not as traumatic as I imagined it might be, and I avoided a pat down and the embarrassment of someone discovering my adult diapers.

Because I don't care that the packaging says they are discrete and look like real underwear: they really don't. Especially if I've been unable to make it to the bathroom the second the urge to pee has struck. And, because of my overactive bladder, it strikes often.

Unfortunately, between the long car trip from Brisbane Airport to Noosa, which took almost two hours with traffic, and then the booking problem at reception, the protection I was wearing did its job, but it was on the verge of leakage by the time we finally made it into the hotel room.

I hate that feeling. Physically and emotionally.

The dampness is uncomfortable, as is the weight of the padding once it gets soaked and puffs up. But then there's the shame of knowing I couldn't hold it. That I've got the bladder control of a toddler. I feel small and vulnerable when it happens; feelings compounded by ex-lovers who said they could handle it but, ultimately, could not.

I can't even blame them. I'm a forty-one-year-old gay man with erectile dysfunction (also caused by surgical complications), no prostate to play with, and I piss myself on the regular.

I am nobody's idea of a catch.

Alex made that perfectly clear when everything fell to shit, too. *Stop thinking about it.*

Sighing, I pull on the new pair of pants and rummage under the bathroom sink for a spare trash can liner. There are three of the little plastic bags there, so I grab one and stuff the old diaper inside, tying it off tightly and, with a grimace, tossing it inside my suitcase to dispose of down the floor's trash chute later. I don't need the incriminating evidence lying around for *Doctor* Aaron Park to discover. I would die of embarrassment.

After getting my cargo pants back on, I check my reflection in the mirror, confirming that the bulk and bagginess conceals my secret. Then I roll my suitcase out of the bathroom, with its bright white tiles and light-colored timber accents, to check out the rest of the apartment.

"I hope you don't mind that I picked my room already," Aaron says from behind me as I poke my head into an open doorway. "They're pretty much identical."

"It's your apartment," I step into the free bedroom as he trails in behind me, "I'm just grateful to have a room at all."

And it is a very nice room. With a king-sized bed and floor-to-ceiling windows looking out over the inviting blue ocean, I can't possibly complain about my lodgings.

"I also turned the A/C on to the most arctic setting I could," Aaron continues. "If it's too cold, let me know. I'm still not completely acclimatized to the Australian summer heat."

I snort. "I'd be happier if you could make it snow inside, so however cold you can get it is perfect for me." My gaze drifts back to the window and I sigh.

The beach looks amazing with its miles of uninterrupted soft sand and gently rolling waves. But hiding my condition is even harder to do in swimwear or shorts, so I will content myself to look from afar. I've never really liked the beach anyway. It's just harder to remember that when it is *right there*.

"It's going to suck going back home," Aaron says, following my gaze. "I live in a landlocked city a few hours east of Cali. Getting to the beach is...a lot."

I nod. "Me too. But I'm not usually a beach person, so..."

"You're not a beach person?" he asks dubiously, turning his head towards the window with a frown. "So you organized a weeklong vacation at a beach resort."

"My best friend did. This is her misguided attempt to get me 'out there' again, or something." Shoulders sagging, I confess, "My last breakup was kind of brutal, but I've stayed single for too long, according to her. My birthday was a few weeks ago and she sprang this whole trip on me as a birthday surprise. The thought was nice, but…"

His appreciative whistle cuts into my trailed off sentence. "That's one generous friend you've got."

Thinking of Bianca, I smile. "She's a generous person. Impulsive, but generous." Casting him a sidelong glance, I muse, "You'd probably get along well."

Aaron's chuckle is low and sexy. "You're not suggesting that my offer to share my room was impulsive, are you?"

Grinning, I nod, "And generous."

The hint of a blush dusts his sharp cheekbones before he clears his throat. "I like helping people."

"That goes hand-in-hand with the doctor thing, I guess." Tilting my head, I ask, "What kind of doctor are you?"

"Nothing specialized. I guess I'm what you'd call a general practitioner. I work in the emergency department of my local hospital, though, so I see a lot of interesting cases."

I snort. "How many of them are 'I was naked, and I accidentally sat on the phallic shaped object' cases?"

He groans, giving his head a shake. "*Way* more than there should be." I snicker as he follows up with: "What about you?"

"I don't deal with inappropriately used household items, no."

Now it's his turn to laugh. The sound lights me up from the inside, and the emergence of a dimple in his left cheek makes my stomach flip. "That's not what I meant." He cocks his head. "What do you do for work?"

"I work for a lifestyle magazine," I shrug, as though my role isn't that important. I'm the EIC, so I'm responsible for the entire publication, and I report solely to the publisher.

Since we began transitioning to digital, with print copies dropping in sales over the past decade, my job has focused more on keeping up with trends and encouraging the editorial team to find niche content than it has on anything else.

However, I still insist on doing a final proofread and edit of most of our content before it goes live. It's my ass on the line if we release anything subpar. While I'm on vacation, that job falls on my deputy's shoulders. Jonathan is even stricter than I am, so woe betide any of the content writers if they think my vacation means they can slack off.

"Oh," Aaron sounds genuinely fascinated, "are you going to use this trip as inspiration for an article?"

It's a fair question, but it's been a long time since I've written any content for our publications. I shake my head. "Nah, this is a work-free zone."

"Amen to that." He offers his fist for a fist bump and then starts to back out of the room, gesturing to my suitcase. "I'll let you unpack and get settled. Just treat this room as you would have your own private booking. Come and go as you please, feel free to bring up any, uh, *new friends* you make." He winks.

My cheeks burn. "You, um, you don't have to worry about that. I'm not..." I sigh. "I can't do hookups. But, obviously, don't let me being in your spare room stop you from bringing anyone up, either."

Frown lines develop in his forehead, but he doesn't press me on the issue. "Okay, well, if you need to get in touch with me, I'll give you my number, too. I was lazy and decided to just pay for international roaming."

"Me too," I nod and pull my phone from my pocket. I haven't checked it in a while, and I can see a text from Bianca on the screen, telling me to enjoy myself.

I'll reply to her later.

We exchange numbers and then Aaron leaves me to do my thing.

While I unpack, cringing at the trash I still need to take out, I sigh again and mull over our conversation.

I wish I could be normal. I wish I could hook up with hot guys whenever the urge strikes. But that means needing to warn guys about my various issues and I find that really difficult to do with strangers. Hell, I can't even do it with close friends, and I'm not trying to sleep with them.

Alex was probably right. I'm too high maintenance.

I should just give up on fantasizing completely and acknowledge that my future is probably going to be one of singledom. And, honestly, there's nothing wrong with being single. I love the independence and freedom of making all my own choices. But sometimes that gets exhausting, and I do get lonely.

That's what I have friends for, I remind myself, grabbing my phone to reply to Bianca's text. *Friends and sex toys. What more could a man really need?*

Chapter Four

Aaron

"**H**ey," I tap lightly on the doorframe to Rowan's room, offering him a smile when he looks up from his reclined position on the bed. I interrupted him texting someone, but he sets the phone down on the mattress beside him and looks at me expectantly. Throwing my thumb over my shoulder, I say, "I'm going to go check out the resort. Want to come with?"

He scrunches his nose in contemplation, and I can't help but think it's a cute expression. He's older and broader than me, but he doesn't carry himself with the kind of confidence (or arrogance) most men who look like him do. Instead, he seems to withdraw into himself, hunching those broad shoulders as if he's trying to shrink and fade into the background.

"I think I'll pass," he replies, and I try not to feel too disappointed at the rejection. "I'm kind of wiped, so I might take a nap. But," his teeth sink into his lower lip, "if you want to join me for dinner later, I'd like that. My treat. For, y'know" —he gestures around the room— "this."

The Daddy in me wants to argue with him about who will be paying, but just because my instincts are screaming that this big, attractive man is submissive, it doesn't mean I can automatically slide into that role with him. So, I smile and tell him, "Sure. I'd like that, too." Glancing at my watch, I say, "I'll probably be back in a few hours, so...dinner around seven?"

His shoulders relax. "Perfect."

***

After exploring the resort and making a mental list of all the things I want to try over the next few days, I head back up to the suite. I almost swallow my tongue when I walk in to find Rowan dressed in loose-cut jeans, and a tight black t-shirt which hugs his biceps and pecs like a second skin.

"Whoa," I breathe, and he arches an eyebrow at me.

I gesture at his outfit, wishing the jeans were just as flattering as the shirt. "You look fantastic."

His cheeks turn pink, and he shakes his head. "Hardly, but thank you."

I want to push the issue, but that might make things weird, so I just roll my eyes. "Give me twenty to grab a quick shower, and I'll be good to go, too."

I dress more casually in beige shorts and a white t-shirt, sliding my bare feet into brown boat shoes. I enjoy the way Rowan's gaze travels over me when I emerge from the bathroom, a glint of appreciation and hunger in his eyes before he blinks it away.

"So," I cock my head, "want to eat here at the resort, or would you like to venture out and explore a bit? I heard some of the guys saying that there are some nice places to eat on Hastings Street. That's, like, the main tourist strip here, I think."

"It could be nice to leave the grounds and see what else is out there. Now that the sun is going down, I don't feel like I'm as likely to melt."

I want to tell him that wearing jeans probably isn't helping with the heat, but he would know that. He's a grown man, and he's not my Boy, so I don't have the right to dress him or even offer suggestions on his clothing. I guess I got too used to picking Jerry's outfits for him.

I pocket my room key, phone, and wallet, and watch as he does the same before we head out of the room together.

We get an Uber from the resort to the main tourist strip, which is a long street of clothing stores, hotels, and restaurants with the main beach on one side and a river running along the other side. It's bustling with people, with a number still flocking to the beach, despite the waning sunlight. Even in summer here, the sun sets around 6:30pm, which is kind of different to back home. It makes the days feel shorter, even though the heat carries on during the night.

Meanwhile, other people are stumbling their way off the sand and onto the sidewalk, their skin damp with salty seawater, granules of sand clinging to them. Some carry surfboards, some have towels draped over their shoulders. Then there are those dressed like me and Rowan, ambling towards the bars and restaurants.

The atmosphere here is somehow both vibrant and relaxed. Most people are smiling, clearly enjoying a vacation themselves, and everything looks bright and airy.

"Want to wander a bit and see if anything calls to us, or have you already Googled and you know exactly what you'd like to eat?"

I ask, guessing that my companion is probably the latter kind of traveler.

He smiles sheepishly. "Usually, I would do that. But this is a thank you meal for you, so...let's see what's out there and then decide?"

Once again, I'm struck by the firm belief that he's quite submissive, and I wonder if he wants me to make the decision because he finds it stressful to make any himself.

"That sounds good to me."

We stroll along the beachfront side of the street first, reading the menus encased behind glass on fancy stands outside each of the restaurants we pass. Seafood seems to be a common theme, which isn't really a surprise, given the location. There's also a little Italian restaurant, and a Mexican one as well, but as we turn around at the end of the street and make our way back on the opposite side, it seems like Rowan and I are on the same page when it comes to our options.

"I like the sound of this place," I say, pointing at the menu of a restaurant midway on our journey back up the street, "or the first one we saw."

"Mmm," he hums agreeably, "me too."

"Do you have a preference between the two?"

He chews his bottom lip, then glances over his shoulder in the direction of the first restaurant we looked at. "The one over there has oceanfront tables...and they had a miso salmon thing on the menu which sounded amazing."

"That did sound good," I agree. "Let's check these last few places while we make our way back to that first one."

There are a bevy of options, but we still find our way back to the first restaurant with its dining room more an open deck jutting out towards the sand and the rolling waves. Despite not having a reservation, we're lucky enough to land ourselves a table for two with uninhibited views, and the salty breeze ruffles our hair as we take our seats.

"Wow," Rowan says, looking out at the darkening ocean instead of at his menu, "this is gorgeous."

The overhead fairy lights have lit up, strung in a zigzag pattern over the large deck, and they glint gold in his wide blue eyes. "Yeah," I agree, "it is."

Rowan smiles and looks down at the menu before he abruptly shifts in his seat. He glances over his shoulder, eyes searching the interior room of the restaurant for something before relief flickers over his face.

Setting the menu down over his plate, he apologizes, "Excuse me for a moment," then pushes away from the table.

I watch as he weaves his way past other diners and disappears inside. At first, I think he's heading towards the bar, but he bypasses it for the bathrooms.

While he's gone, a waitress appears to take our drink order. I glance at the wine list and choose each of us a glass of white wine from what the menu says is a local vineyard, hoping that I'm not overstepping by choosing for my companion.

He slides back into his seat only moments before the waitress returns with the drinks.

"I hope you don't mind," I say softly. "I have this thing where I like to try local stuff when I travel."

Rowan shakes his head, locks of brown hair falling into his eyes before he brushes them back with his hand. "Not at all. I try to do that, too." He lifts his glass. "To...new experiences?"

I grin. "I'll drink to that."

***

Dinner with Rowan feels like a date, but in the best possible way. We discover that we live in the same city back home, which is a wild coincidence given how far from home we both are, and we share similar tastes in fiction, TV, and even food. When our meals are delivered to our table, Rowan catches me eyeing his salmon dish and he smiles shyly, nudging his plate forward.

"We could share both?" he suggests, his eyes greedily taking in the swordfish sashimi on my plate.

There's something so sweet and wholesome in the way he offers to share that my stomach gives a funny little flip-flop. "Are you sure?" I ask.

He nods, pushing his meal even further into the middle of the table. "Please. It's been a long time since I've done this with anyone."

"Me too," I lift my cutlery and cut into the salmon, being sure to swish my piece through the miso glace, "Jerry wasn't a sharer."

"Not everyone is," he says, watching as I pop the forkful of food into my mouth. My tastebuds dance at the explosion of flavor and I moan, making him chuckle. "But I like seeing other people happy. I like sharing in that, too, I guess."

I chew thoughtfully, mulling over the quiet confession. Swallowing, I dip my chin, "Well, Jerry was a spoiled brat, and I enabled him." I gesture to his plate. "But that is *so* good. You have to try it."

Rowan cuts himself a corner from his end of the piece of fish, using the side of his fork to slice through the tender meat. I watch the utensil slip between his parted lips and my stomach flips again as his eyes flutter shut with his enjoyment of the food.

Yeah; I've definitely missed this.

In fact, if we weren't complete strangers, I would get another forkful of the melt-in-your-mouth salmon and feed it to him myself, just to feel even more responsible for his sheer pleasure.

Getting a bit creepy, Park. Reel it in.

Lifting the set of chopsticks that came with my meal, I dive in to the sashimi to distract myself from those intrusive thoughts.

I can't help the fact that there's something about Rowan calling out to my Daddy instincts. It's nothing I can put my finger on, but he just seems...Little. And lost. Lonely.

Alliteration. Well done.

The voice in my head is snarky tonight.

Rowan tries the sashimi after me, and we compare how fresh and light the dish is, compared to the comfort and warmth of the salmon meal. Neither of us can pick a favorite, but we do agree that we need to have dessert afterwards.

"Here, or from the gelato place down the street?" I ask.

He shrugs. "I don't mind, I—" His eyes widen and his body tenses up, his shoulders and spine going rigid. A pink flush dusts over his cheeks.

"Are you okay?" I ask, leaning forward. "Were you allergic to something in the food, or—"

"No. No. I just...Excuse me."

He pushes back from the table and hurries towards the bathrooms again, and I frown at his retreating back. I wonder if the meal didn't agree with him, or whether jetlag has messed with his constitution. My concern grows the longer he's away from the table.

Should I follow him?

Both the doctor in me and the Daddy seem to think I should.

When the waitress swings by to collect our empty dishes, I assure her that everything was amazing, and I ask for the check. Rowan still hasn't resurfaced by the time I've paid for the meal, and that is enough to allow my concern to override my fears of crossing a line.

I weave my way through the still-crowded restaurant and into the bathrooms. The men's room has three stalls, but only one is occupied, and there isn't anyone at the urinals. Closing the main door and sliding the lock across to guarantee a modicum of privacy, I step up to the far stall door and tap on it.

"Rowan?"

There's a hitch of breath, then a defeated, "Sorry."

That does nothing to ease my worries. "Sorry? Why sorry? Are you all right? Did the meal not agree?"

"No," there's a wobble to his voice that brings Daddy Aaron ever-closer to the surface. "No, my stomach is fine. I...I just...I...Fuck, you'd think after twenty years this would get easier, but it never does, and—"

"Sweetheart," I cut him off, hearing the wobble in his voice escalating into panic, "you're working yourself up. Breathe for me."

His breathing is shaky, before he quietly pleads, "I just want to go home."

There's something incredibly heartbreaking in the way the words come out, his voice clogged with tears and...shame? He might not be aware of it, but he sounds so young and helpless, it tugs at my heartstrings.

"We can do that," I tell him, aware that I've dipped into the soothing Daddy voice I reserved for Jerry's meltdowns. "We'll go back to the resort and—"

"N-no," he sounds so broken, "I want to go *home*. I sh-should never have come here. I...I miss my house, and cold weather, and s-sweaters..."

"Rowan, honey, breathe." I have no idea what has triggered this, but every instinct in me screams to comfort him and fix it. "Can I come in?"

He's silent for a long moment. Then there's some shuffling and the latch over the handle of the stall door turns from the red 'occupied' sign to the green 'vacant' one. The door swings inwards, and Rowan stands in front of me, his eyes downcast.

He's slightly taller than me, and certainly bulkier, but he's once again doing his best to shrink into himself.

"Sweetheart, what's" —he lifts his hand at his side, holding an item I'm intimately familiar with, and gently eases past me to drop it into the trashcan in the corner of the room, where it lands with a telling *thud*— "wrong?" I finish, though the wet patch on the back of his jeans, dark blue over light denim, answers my question for me.

For a moment, we stand in silence, the only sounds coming from him washing his hands and sniffling.

Then I come to my damn senses.

"Rowan, baby, look at me."

His face is bright red, his embarrassment more than obvious, and he cringes as he complies, speaking before I get a chance to try and assure him that it'll be okay. "I...it's a medical thing. I...I know I'm d-disgusting, but—"

"What?"

"I...I must have...the wine...I..." He closes his eyes, and I watch his Adam's apple bob almost violently. "Alex always said my bladder can't handle wine. Guess he was right about that, too."

I'd bet the Rolex my dad gave me when I graduated from med school that Alex is also the reason this sweet man thinks he's 'disgusting'. I want five minutes alone with this Alex. I swear, I just want to talk. With my fists. And not like a cute puppet show.

"Firstly," I tell him, firmly but calmly, "You are not disgusting. I can understand why incontinence can be embarrassing at times, but you are *not* disgusting. I need to hear you repeat that."

Bewildered, red-rimmed, wet eyes flash upwards to meet mine. "What?"

"Repeat it."

"I'm not disgusting," he mumbles.

"Good boy," the praise slips out, but I stand by it, "because you are not."

"But—"

"It's just pee, Rowan. We all pee."

"Yeah, well, most people manage to make it to the bathroom."

I want to tell him that some people *enjoy* not making it, but I don't think he's ready to hear that right now. Not while we're standing in this men's room, anyway. Later, when he's calmed down, I want to try to undo some of the damage this Alex person has done.

Instead, in response to his self-deprecating snark, I say, "You did everything you could to mitigate that. Sometimes, protection fails."

"Pretty sure that's how I came into existence," he mutters.

I snort. "Me too, to be honest." Not that my parents were anything less than loving and supportive, but I'm sure they thought they were done and dusted with my older siblings —the youngest of whom was nine when I came about— when I appeared. Still, my words do the trick and the corner of Rowan's plump lips ticks upwards. Relieved, I smile and softly tell him, "We can fix this. Do you trust me?"

Chapter Five

Dinner was going *so* well. So, naturally, I managed to fuck it up. Or, rather, my body did. I was so careful, too. I mean, okay, when I went to the bathroom at the start of dinner, I discovered that I must have wet without realizing it, but it hadn't been enough to worry about. Usually, I get enough warning that I need to go that, if I'm at a restaurant, I can make it in time.

It must have been the wine. For some reason, wine goes through me faster than most liquids, and I didn't get the usual pang from my bladder before I felt the leakage into my jeans.

In the bathroom, I'd hoped I could minimize the impact somehow, but it was too late and too noticeable. I didn't even have a sweater with me to wrap around my waist to hide my shame.

Stupid tropical climate.

But now Aaron is standing in front of me, far calmer and kinder than any stranger in his position needs to be, and his question hangs between us as he waits for my reply.

Do I trust him? I barely know him.

But he hasn't freaked out at the fact that you wet your pants like a toddler, the voice in my head argues. *He hasn't run out of the restaurant and left you to deal with this on your own.*

I'd almost convinced myself that our dinner felt romantic. Like a date. Knowing that, against all odds, we live in the same city back home made it seem almost like the universe was telling me to move on.

Then...the accident happened.

And Aaron stayed. He came looking for you. He offered you a room to stay in for no good reason.

Licking my lips, I nod. "I trust you."

His answering smile brings out his dimple, and he nods. "Good boy," he murmurs, stepping into my personal space. The strange endearment makes my belly feel fizzy, but in a good way. "I'm going to take your jeans off, okay? The main door is locked; it's just us here."

My heart immediately begins to beat faster and harder, the shame of the situation slamming back into me, but he seems ready for it. Splaying his hand over my chest —right over my thumping heart— he shushes me. "I'll only need them for a couple of minutes, okay? You can go sit in the stall, see if your bladder has anything else to give, and by the time you're done, these will be dry."

I can't explain it, but there's something in the way he speaks that just calms me right down, and it feels *good* to hand over the reins and responsibility of dealing with this to someone else. I know I shouldn't —it's my mess to clean up, my problem to resolve— but the relief of being told what to do makes my head feel light.

"Okay," I answer, allowing him to undo the button and fly, stepping out of each leg at his instruction.

With a bare ass on display, I make my way back into the toilet stall and will my bladder to cooperate. If I empty it again now, I'll stay dry for the return trip to the hotel.

The sound of the air hand dryer starts up while I think of running water, and I understand immediately what Aaron is doing for me. In my panic, I never would have thought to do the same.

When I'm sure I've done all I can to ensure a dry trip back to the resort, I flush the toilet and head over to wash my hands again. Aaron grins and pulls my jeans away from the hand dryer while I reach for paper towels.

"Tada," he declares, holding them out for me, "all fixed. They might be a bit warm when you put them on, so give it a few seconds."

I avert my gaze, shyness and renewed embarrassment worming away in my stomach, but I still murmur my thanks as I take my jeans and climb back into them. It's a relief knowing that I can walk out of here with my head up.

"All good?" Aaron asks, and I nod. He holds out his hand for me to take, and I barely hesitate to do so. "Let's get going."

***

The trip back to the resort is practically silent. I can't bring myself to say anything with a third party in the car, but I know that I won't want to talk about it when we get back to the room, anyway.

Nevertheless, Aaron's shoulders are loose and relaxed, and he sits beside me in the back seat of the Uber, reaching out to squeeze my thigh in what I take as a reassuring gesture. But then he leaves his hand there for the entire trip, a comforting weight, almost allowing me to believe that I'm not alone in dealing with my issues anymore.

But that is a dangerous line of thinking. He's young. He can —and should— do better than me. He deserves better than me. In fact, most everyone does. I'm too much. Situations like tonight? They're too much to expect anyone to deal with on a regular basis.

And what if someone else had wanted to use the bathroom while we had it locked? What if they'd thought we were…I don't know…having sex or something in there? What if they'd called the police, or broken the lock to get in, or—

"Sweetheart, breathe," Aaron's voice is low and soothing. He guides me through the rising anxiety by modeling deep breaths in and out for me. His hand never leaves my thigh.

"Can you talk to me about what triggered your panic attack just now?" he asks after we've climbed out of the Uber. He gives me time to consider whether I want to as we climb the steps to the foyer and cross the glossy tiled floor.

Cringing, I eventually admit, "I overthink things sometimes. When I'm already stressed, it gets worse, and I start spiraling over all the things that could have gone even more wrong. I know I'm dumb to—"

"Our brains can be dumb sometimes, not us." Aaron's interruption is a gentle rebuke. "We can't always control the way we think or the thoughts we have, especially when we're already highly emotional." He stops to face me as we wait for the elevator. "You're not dumb for having thoughts like that. You know that, right?"

"Alex used to say—"

"I get the feeling your Alex did a number on you, so forgive me, but I am going to put zero stock in anything he…they?…said to you. Ever."

I snort.

There's nobody else around us, but I can hear music drifting in faintly from the direction of the hotel bar-slash-nightclub on the other side of the building. Lady Gaga's *Bad Romance* tickles my brain. What is the universe trying to tell me now?

"He," I nod as the elevator opens in front of us. I wait for Aaron to walk in ahead of me. "And, yeah, okay…referencing anything he used to say is probably pointless. He was a dick." Leaning against the cool, mirrored wall, I sigh. "We were together for a few years. It's hard to let go of some of the things ingrained in me from that. Especially when it was my issues that ended us."

"Sweetheart," Aaron's expression falls, and there's a hint of horror in his voice, "*no*. I doubt that."

The doors ding open on the fourth floor and we step out as I bristle, "You've known me for less than a day."

"Fine," he rolls his eyes. "Did you end your relationship? You dumped him? Broke his heart?" Reaching into his pocket as we reach our door, he swipes his card over the reader then twists the door handle, his eyebrows raised expectantly for my answer.

"Well," I step inside at his gesture, "no, but I know that being with me —a neurotic, incontinent homebody with erectile dysfunction— isn't exactly winning the boyfriend lottery. We couldn't do the things he wanted, I was embarrassing, I—"

"Those are *his* issues, not yours." Aaron closes the door and strides across to the couch in the main living area, sitting down and patting the spot beside him. "You didn't do anything wrong by existing, Rowan. I'm coming at this as an unbiased outsider with a medical degree: I *know* men in your position do everything they can to minimize their symptoms and the severity of their conditions, and I am sure you are the same. If Alex couldn't handle it, that's on him."

It's funny. In my own head, I *know* Alex was self-centered and a bit of a prick. But when it comes to talking about it, I always find myself rationalizing the things he said or did. Bianca's called me out on it a number of times, not that she knows *why* he always used to be so frustrated with me or embarrassed by me, but hearing Aaron defend me from the pains of my last relationship is validating in a completely unexpected way.

"Yeah...you're right. I know you are," I tell him. "I just...I have moments like tonight, and it throws me off-kilter. And it reminds me that I'm better off single. Not that...not that that was a date. And, oh God, I didn't even get to pay after everything that happened."

Aaron shakes his head, reaching out to grasp my hand in his. His hands are big and warm. Grounding. He squeezes gently. "It was the best date I've been on in a while," he says. "Whether it was supposed to be or not."

Wait...what?

The realization that I'm still wearing the same jeans I wet earlier hits me hard and I push to my feet, abruptly ending whatever *that* was. Aaron Park is far too good to wind up with me, even for a summer fling. "I'm going to go shower and change. You, um, you didn't have to help me tonight, but you did, and I appreciate that."

He also stands up, reaching for me. "Rowan..."

"No, I...I feel gross, and I'd better change and..."

"I'm a Daddy," he blurts.

"I...sorry, what?"

Lifting his hand to run long, elegant fingers through thick black hair, he sighs. "I'm a Daddy. A kink Daddy. A soft Dom, too, I guess. I...The reason I originally booked a two-bedroom suite was because my ex and I wanted a nursery away from home. Somewhere to store his toys and" —he looks meaningfully at me— "change his diapers."

My heart starts to race. "*What?*"

"I'm into age play. ABDL...have you heard of it?"

"In porn, yeah." I am aware that I still sound bewildered. "But I didn't...you mean people actually dress up as babies in reality?"

Aaron nods. "It's not just about the kink, though. It's...there's this whole give and take with trust and vulnerability and a level of intimacy and connection that is really hard to put into words. It...it doesn't have to be sexual, but, I mean," he rubs the back of his neck, shoulders rising as he confesses, "I'm also kind of into watersports, so..."

"I'm guessing you don't mean the kind with snorkels or flippers."

"I'm not against costumes in the bedroom."

I let out a bark of surprised laughter. Before I know it, I'm sitting down heavily on the couch again. He follows tentatively. "I just...I wanted to tell you in case...well, in case that was something you hadn't considered pursuing before. I've met a couple of guys on the scene who got into it to give some empowerment to their conditions."

"I don't have any interest in dressing like or talking like a baby. I'm not kink shaming, but...that's not for me."

Aaron doesn't seem surprised or even disappointed. Instead, he smiles understandingly. "Well, you can be more on the DL scale than the AB, or vice versa. It really comes down to what makes you happy and comfortable. A good Daddy will work with you to find the right balance."

"A...Daddy." I repeat the word clumsily. It sets off a strange flutter in my stomach.

Sure, I've watched and even read my fair share of Daddy kink, but I've never imagined *calling* someone Daddy before.

"Let me ask you this," he says, "and I want you to answer honestly. When I helped you in the bathroom tonight —when I took over and told you I was going to fix everything— how did you feel?"

"Relieved," the word leaves my lips before I can really process my thoughts. I blush. "Safe. Looked after." Unexpectedly, tears well in my eyes and I blink rapidly to dispel them. He'd called me 'good boy' and I had wanted to hear it again. "I...You made me feel like I didn't have to worry anymore."

His smile isn't smug or even knowing. It's soft and sweet, matching his voice when he reaches for my hand again and says, "Then I did my job as a Daddy right. And, if you'd be okay with it, maybe that's something we could keep doing together?"

I blink. "You...you want to be my Daddy?"

He nods.

I should say no. I should ask him if he's out of his mind. I'm a stranger. Not only that, but I'm a stranger who, up until two minutes ago, thought Adult Baby Diaper Loving stuff was just a porn thing.

But the words out of my mouth aren't any of the above. No. When I open my mouth, only one word comes out.

"Why?"

Chapter Six

Aaron

Why.

It's a loaded question with a loaded answer.

Honestly, I could have —*should have*— tried to raise the topic with more tact, but I'd felt my chance slipping away. Since helping Rowan in the restaurant bathroom, the attraction I'd felt during our impromptu date had turned into some kind of attachment. It's hard for me to not get attached when I'm in Daddy mode. It's why the age play is a lifestyle thing for me, and why I don't usually go for just scene play.

But, like most Daddies, I'm adaptive to the needs of my Boys. I don't need my Boys to regress super young, and if they do regress but aren't into diapers, that's also okay. Like I told Rowan, it's all about finding the balance that makes both partners happy. And the thing that makes me most happy is taking care of my Boys in whatever capacity they need.

Though, I will be honest; it's always a bonus to find a partner who is into diaper play, if not watersports. They're not things I *have* to have in my relationships, but they add an extra level of enjoyment for me.

So having a hot as fuck man whose needs tick all my boxes practically land in my lap is something I honestly can't just ignore. I had to shoot my shot.

But how do I succinctly explain all of that without sounding like a bit of a creeper? I mean, the poor guy has gone through a lot today and I don't want him to think I'm taking advantage while he's vulnerable. I also don't want him to think that I'm only suggesting this because he's convenient, because that's not the case, either.

I really like Rowan. Aside from being gorgeous, he's sweet and funny, and our date tonight (even if it wasn't supposed to be one) was perfect. We never ran out of topics of conversation, and I still want to keep getting to know him. I genuinely think we could be good for each other.

In the end, I lay it all on the table. I explain that my love of helping people is what led me to a career as a doctor, but also what drives me as a Daddy.

There's a wry twist to his lips as he takes it all in. The smirk under that salt and pepper stubble is like catnip to me. "So...my fucked-up issues appeal to you as both a Daddy and a...sub?"

"I prefer to say Boy instead of sub," I answer the latter half of his question first, before shaking my head. "But you're not fucked up, Rowan. For the record, I thought you were hot when I was checking you out at the concierge's desk."

"Yeah...now that makes your offer to share the room kinda' creepy," he teases.

I still take the bait. "I told you — I'm impulsive and I like to help people."

"This whole 'let me be your Daddy' thing is definitely lining up with the impulsive thing, I'll give you that."

It's a good sign that he's being sassy, right? That he's flirting instead of freaking out?

Holding my hands in surrender, I concede, "Guilty as charged. I didn't mean to just word-vomit that out tonight. But the idea snuck into my head, and I wanted to put it out there. The room is still yours if you say no, by the way."

"Can I think about it? Sleep on it, even? I've never let anyone even see the diapers before, let alone...y'know."

"Change them?"

His cheeks are pink. God, he's cute.

"Yeah. I...I don't know..." Exhaling, he scrubs his hand over his face. "What other kinds of things would be involved in the kinky side? If I did agree to try it, I mean."

"Whatever you're comfortable with. It really could just be as simple as calling me Daddy when we make out or go to bed. No dress-ups, no toys or regression, none of that. And I wouldn't change you without your explicit consent."

"Right." He cocks his head. "So, like...dating, but calling you Daddy during sexy times?" I nod. He bites his lip. "You mentioned watersports."

"Again, it's not something we *have* to do, but I don't mind being the recipient of a golden shower," I shrug. "And I get that that can be confronting, so you could also sit on my lap while wearing your incontinence pants and...let go."

He inhales sharply and squirms, the pinkness of his cheeks now fiery red. "That's...I mean, I can't imagine why..."

I shrug again. I don't mind explaining why I enjoy it. It might help him while he mulls over his options. "Everyone's got these kinks for various reasons. For me, it's multifaceted. There's obviously something kind of taboo about it, which gives it a bit of a thrill. But it's also super intimate. Both parties are being really vulnerable in those moments, but in different ways, and the trust required goes both ways, too. Then there's the pure physical enjoyment of the heat and wetness and the rush of being so free of rules and expectations...Plus, like I said, there are guys like you who do it because it makes them feel more in control of losing that control, you know?"

Biting his lip, Rowan seems to be really taking it all in. "And, in an ideal, um, Daddy/Boy arrangement, what would *you* really like to do together? If you had carte blanche and knew the, um, the Boy would be happy with all of it?"

"Well," I muse, wanting to be completely honest, "like I said, my biggest things are helping my Boy and making sure he's happy. I guess in my previous relationships, that's involved diaper play, some regression play, taking over all the stressful decisions for my Boys in their day-to-day lives outside of work...that kind of thing."

"Okay," his expression doesn't give anything about his feelings on my answer away. But he definitely looks and sounds more guarded when he asks, "And sex? Are you a strict top?"

"I'm vers, actually. Very happily, too."

"And if you had a Boy who doesn't like bottoming? Would that be okay for a week? A year? However long you saw the relationship going?"

"Of course," my answer doesn't need any thought. "My College boyfriend was a strict side and that was one of the hottest relationships I've ever had." I sigh. "We weren't suited for each other for different reasons, and we split up amicably, by the way."

"Good to know," the words are back to light and playful, but then he stiffens and pushes back to his feet.

"Sorry, I..." he throws his thumb over his shoulder, and I wave him off.

"Go. Have your shower." It's on the tip of my tongue to offer to get him fresh clothes, but the ball is firmly in his court, and I won't push this any more than I already have. "I'm going to head to bed and read."

He checks his watch, then arches an eyebrow at me. "Read? You don't want to go check out the club or anything?"

Shaking my head, I offer him a lopsided smile. "I'm not a huge partier. Plus, it's been a long day" —longer for him, I'm aware— "so I'm just gonna wind down. If you need me, you know where to find me."

He nods, then hustles into the bathroom.

I know I've given him a lot to think about.

Chapter Seven

Rowan

The hot water is cleansing and seeps into my muscles, easing the tension that's been building in my shoulders and back since I got on the flight here. Tears gather in the corners of my eyes even as the relief sweeps over me.

I always get emotional when I'm tired.

And I am beyond tired right now. It's been a long couple of days with very little sleep, and today was an emotional rollercoaster of epic proportions.

I can't believe I told a complete stranger how messed up I am.

I can't believe he's into it.

I'm not sure how to feel about the revelation that Aaron is not only not turned off by my incontinence, but that he's actually more interested in me because of it. I would never judge anyone for their kinks, but I wasn't expecting a straight-laced doctor to be into diapers and watersports, or to be so open and upfront about it.

The honesty and lack of shame is intriguing, though. Refreshing.

After a lifetime of feeling flawed and broken, of hiding this part of me I literally can't control, hearing such an openly positive perspective on it has my stomach flipping and fluttering with anticipation and hope.

That feels more dangerous than his kindness.

I can't afford to get attached to the idea of someone liking this part of me. Not just tolerating it but *liking* it. If Alex was able to destroy my confidence, imagine what letting go of someone who professes to like my issues might do to me.

But I can't help remembering how amazing it felt to be taken care of in that restaurant bathroom. When he took control of the situation. When he made everything better.

Imagine having that all the time.

My throat tightens and the tears slide down my cheeks, mingling with the shower's spray.

I shouldn't let myself want it. It's easier being alone. It's easier to not risk another loss and more pain.

But Bianca was right. I *am* lonely.

Aaron's offering an end to that loneliness.

He's a gorgeous man. Intelligent, kind, generous...he's well and truly out of my league.

Except there's a voice in my head that sounds suspiciously like my best friend telling me that I should look at the way things have come together. The entire comedy of errors which saw me sharing a suite with this stranger. Learning that we live in the same city back home. Then, to top that off, learning that my biggest flaws —the things that make me undatable to most men— play right into his kinks.

If I did believe in signs from the universe, these would all be neon, flashing ones.

I'm going to regret it forever if I don't give it a chance, aren't I?

***

"You can do this," I tell myself as I hover outside Aaron's bedroom door. I'm wearing nothing but a towel, and I'm feeling equal parts excited and nervous. At worst case, if this turns out to be a mistake, I can just book myself a hotel room somewhere else and get an Uber there, and call this entire vacation a mistake, like I originally thought it would be. I take a deep breath and stare at the painted white door. "Just...knock."

My hand trembles as I raise it, but before I can lose my nerve, I rap my knuckles quickly and softly.

My heart races in the seconds that follow, and I'm already considering fleeing to my bedroom when the door swings open. Aaron's gaze travels over my towel-clad form before resting on my face.

"What's up?" he asks lightly, and I struggle to find the words to express exactly what I want.

"I was...I mean, are you...*Can* you..." It's all a jumble in my head, embarrassment creeping up my spine and crawling over my cheeks. I swallow, forcing myself to breathe and to use my words. "I thought about it," I tell him, gripping the towel around my waist with clammy hands, "and...I want to try it. If you still want to, I mean. All of it. I liked being looked after and, yeah, it might be weird to have another grown man put me in a diaper, but...I'm so tired, Aaron. I'm tired, and lonely, and what you said sounded really nice."

"Oh, sweetheart, come here," he pulls me in for a hug, my warm, damp skin pressed up against his thin cotton t-shirt.

The steady thumping of his heart against mine is more soothing than I could ever have imagined it would be. He rubs his hand over my back, making soft shushing sounds, and I just melt into him.

"Are you sure you want to start tonight?" he asks, his voice a pleasant murmur against my ear.

I nod. "Please. I...It's been so long since anyone touched me...since...since someone wasn't revolted by me and..." I pause to swallow against the lump in my throat, blinking back more traitorous tears. "I Googled a bit when I got out of the shower, and it sounds doable. Good, even. Being cherished by someone. Being someone's priority. I haven't had that in a long time. And...if it's only going to be for this week..."

"Let's sit and talk about that, okay?" he suggests, but it sounds more like he has already decided for me, and the rush of relief I feel from that small act alone tells me that I'm making the right decision here.

"I just need to get dressed first. Or at least into my, uh..." Heat flares in my cheeks. I'm not used to talking about my 'special' underwear with anyone, let alone people who have known me for less than a day.

"Do you wear different protection at night?" he asks calmly, while the embarrassment simmers inside me. "It would make sense if you do. If you have an overactive bladder and manage to sleep deeply, wearing extra absorbent incontinence padding is the smarter choice."

He says it with understanding and even a touch of warmth, which eases some of the tightness in my chest. I nod. "I actually wear a proper diaper at night," the admission would usually make me cringe, but it's already easier with him. Maybe because I know that he plays with them for fun? Or because he's a doctor and this is something he comes across professionally? I don't know, but it's nice not to feel quite so anxious about it. "The incontinence underwear wasn't enough. When this all happened, my doctor at the time recommended stuffers as well for extra absorbency and it's...awkward, but it works."

"I'm glad that you've found something to make things easier, though. Changing sheets constantly isn't fun. Especially on your own, I'm sure."

Better than having your bedmate tell you how disgusting and useless you are.

I swallow back the words and nod again.

Aaron guides me into my room and sits me down on the edge of the bed. "Are you okay with me helping with this? I usually rely on the traffic light system with my partners: green for all clear, yellow to pause and discuss hesitancy or any concerns, and red for stop completely. Does that work for you?"

"Yeah," I lick my lips, with the situation suddenly feeling very real. As he hovers over my suitcase, which is on its side on the carpet in the corner, my heart hammers. "And, um, green light. I'm okay with this."

"Just red light if you change your mind, sweetheart, okay?"

He lifts the top lid of my suitcase and zeros in on the packages I reserve for night use only. Grabbing a diaper and a stuffer, he also pulls out a pair of thin pajama pants and a t-shirt for me, too.

"Do you use a barrier cream?" he asks as he sets it all down in a neat pile at my hip.

I know my face is on fire, but I force myself to answer. "Yeah. It's in my toiletries bag. I left it in the bathroom. Sorry, I'll go—"

"Stay put, sweetheart. Daddy's got it."

A thrill of something undefinable shoots through me at his words and I do as he says, sitting quietly as he disappears and returns in less than thirty seconds.

"Okay, lay back for me."

I do as he says, closing my eyes against the intense wave of anticipation and embarrassment that hits me.

But my towel remains in place, even as I feel the gentle brush of his fingers at the knot above my hips.

"Traffic light?" he prompts softly.

It takes me a moment to find my voice. "Green."

The towel is pried open, my body exposed as I recline on the hotel bed. The cool air from the AC is almost like a shock to my sensitive system, but Aaron smooths a warm palm over my left thigh. "Shh," he soothes, "you're doing so well, Ro. You're being a good boy. Thank you for trusting me."

The praise and sweet words go straight to my head, bringing back the light, floaty feeling from earlier. I relax into his touch as he continues to rub over my thighs, and when I hear him fluff out the diaper, I lift my hips without needing to be told.

"That's it," I can hear a smile in his voice, but it sounds encouraging instead of mocking, "good job. You can drop back down now." I do, and I can feel the familiar padding, emphasized by the additional stuffer, under my ass. "I'm going to put the cream on now, baby. Remember your safe words. I'll stop if you want me to."

"Mmmhmm," I agree, though I have no intention of telling him to stop. Not with how gentle he's being. How reverent.

Nobody has ever touched me like this. Like I'm precious.

And that is exactly how it feels as the thick white cream is applied to my skin. Aaron's touch isn't hesitant, but it doesn't feel clinical or rushed, either. It feels like every stroke over my skin is filled with care, like he wants me to know that he understands how important this is to me, and like the whole activity of diapering me is something we should enjoy, rather than just something I have to do.

I almost whine when he stops, but I feel him wiping his hand on the towel before the front of the diaper is held snugly over my sadly flaccid dick. I wish it would spring to life more often, that it would show Aaron just how much I really did enjoy his attention just now. But it's just as defective as my bladder and only works on its own schedule.

By the time he's taped down both sides, I feel more secure in my nighttime protection than I have in decades.

I jolt at the soft press of lips to the inside of my left thigh.

"All done," Aaron says, with a discernible rasp to his voice that was not there earlier.

I feel boneless right now, like I've melded with the mattress, and it's an effort to force my eyes open. But, when I do, I'm rewarded with a sweet smile.

"You did really well, sweetheart," he tells me. "How do you feel?"

My head feels soupy, probably from the exhaustion of the day finally taking over, but I make myself answer. "Good," I manage. "Nice. Sleepy."

He chuckles. "Well, you're not dressed for bed yet, Ro. We still have to get your jammies on."

Jammies.

For all that I said I'm not interested in baby talk or dressing like one, I kind of like these childlike words. They make me feel a bit giggly and bubbly inside, and bring out a more youthful side of me, too.

"Mm'kay," I tell him. "You gonna help?"

If he's surprised by my lapse into simplified vocabulary, he doesn't show it. "Of course, sweetheart. C'mon, sit up."

I grumble as he pulls me back up into a seated position, and fuss as he wrestles me into the t-shirt. Then he steps back and I can't read the expression on his face, but it makes my stomach flip.

"You look fucking adorable right now," he tells me. "How would you feel being left in just your tee and diaper for now?"

I shrug. It's comfortable enough.

He snorts.

"Where's your headspace, sweetheart?" he asks when I don't answer verbally. "Because if I didn't know any better, I'd say you're regressing a bit."

"Mm'tired," I complain in a whine that, yeah, sounds *very* young. If I wasn't quite so tired, I would probably fight to regain my composure. But the pull of snuggling up in my dry, soft outfit and sleeping off the jetlag is too tempting.

"I see," he sounds amused and even fond. "We'll talk about how we both see this thing between us playing out tomorrow, then."

"Good idea," I scramble the reply together. "Can we just cuddle now?"

"Sure, sweetheart. Just let me go hang your towel back up in the bathroom."

This time I do whine in disappointment, but I sigh happily when he returns and climbs onto the bed with me. We spoon together, with him as the big spoon at my back, and the floaty sensation in my head gets more intense.

It's almost like euphoria, and it's a bit sad to realize that I'm so starved for touch and affection that a simple cuddle is making my head spin.

"I'm really proud of you for asking for my help tonight," he says as my eyes get heavier.

"Mmm," is the only reply I can manage.

"You're a sweet Boy, Ro. Thank you for giving me a chance to be your Daddy."

As I allow sleep to take me, the words play over in my head on repeat.

My Daddy.

It's not something I ever thought I wanted, but I can't deny that I'm really starting to like the sound of that.

My Daddy.

Mine.

Chapter Eight

Waking up in the morning, I'm cocooned in warmth. There are arms and legs wrapped around me like an octopus, with warm skin pressed against mine and soft breaths puffing into my chest. I snuggle into it with a satisfied sigh, breathing in the coconut shampoo on the soft hair tickling my nose. My cock stirs in my pajama pants, but I close my eyes, staying sleepy and content.

I want to savor the moment.

It's been a while since Jerry and I last woke up entwined like this. The last time was at least three months ago. We'd already started drifting apart, with him resentful of my shiftwork, and it was at least a month before he told me—

My eyes fly open.

This isn't Jerry.

Memories from yesterday finally filter into my foggy brain as a burst of heat blooms over the top of my thigh, the already squishy diaper against my skin becoming fuller and momentarily warmer. I hold Rowan a bit closer as he fusses and groans in his sleep, rubbing his back to hopefully extend his peacefulness.

Last night was unexpected and perfect. I feel a stab of guilt for thinking about Jerry in those first wakeful moments just now, but it was out of habit more than for emotional reasons. With my brain officially back online, I am happy that Rowan is the man in my arms.

We didn't get to talk about it yesterday, but I hope that this will be more than just a holiday fling. The fact that we live in the same city back home means that it probably can be, assuming Rowan enjoyed last night as much as I did, and that we can discover more compatibility over the coming days.

"Mmm," he mumbles adorably, nuzzling his stubbled cheek against my chest. "Morning."

"Good morning, sweetheart," I reply quietly, pressing a kiss to the top of his head.

He stiffens, his whole body tensing. I shush him as he attempts to pull away, but I don't hold him against his will as he practically wrenches his hips backwards and rolls into the empty space behind him. His cheeks are bright red, and he grabs for the light blanket, covering his lower body.

"Try not to panic," I murmur, "you're safe here. It's all okay."

Rowan's fingers tighten over the blanket clutched over his hips, his knuckles turning white. "I...I need..."

"A change, yeah," I nod, carefully smoothing my hand over his bicep. He's not the sleepy, relaxed, possibly regressed man I helped into the diaper last night, and I don't want to spook him. But I'm not going to tiptoe around this, either. "I can take care of that, sweetheart." He turns startled, wide eyes at me. I respond with an easy smile. "You told me last night that you want to try the Daddy thing, right? This is part of that. What's your traffic light color?"

He cringes, hips moving under the blanket. I assume his protection is sodden and clammy by now. "Yellow."

My hand continues to rub at his bicep. "Okay, let's talk about what you're feeling. What was last night like for you?"

Licking his lips, Rowan admits, "It was good. Weirdly relaxing." The tiny smile he wears from his memories fades away and he squirms again. "But I was dry and clean from the shower last night. Now..."

"You're wet from a deep sleep. That's normal and expected."

He scrunches his nose. "But...it's gross."

"Says who?"

"What?"

"Who says it's gross? It's just pee, Rowan. A quick wipe and you'll be all fresh again."

"But..." he flounders, then sighs. "Everyone else has always thought it was gross."

"Yeah, well, I'm guessing none of your exes were Daddies. For me, this is normal, with or without a medical condition."

He takes a moment to think about it, his fingers flexing and unflexing on the blanket's hem. "You really don't think it's disgusting and weird?"

The vulnerability in his voice breaks my heart. I want to track down every single man who has made him feel like his condition makes him unlovable and cause them irreparable damage. How dare they hurt this beautiful, sweet man over something so harmless?

"Absolutely not." Wanting to lighten the mood, I give him a crooked grin and wave a hand over the erection tenting the soft cotton of my sleep pants. "Case in point: I'm more into being your Daddy than I think you understand."

His gaze drifts down my body and his cheeks flush pink again. "Really?"

"That's more than just morning wood," I confirm. "I *enjoy* all of this, Ro."

There's a suspicious sheen of moisture in his eyes as he looks back at my face almost shyly. "I like that nickname," he says. "Nobody's ever given me one before. Well, okay, Bianca calls me Dumbass, but that's not the same."

I snort and hold my arms open. "C'mere. Come cuddle, then I'll change you."

He only hesitates for a moment before he shuffles back across the bed and into my arms. He fits well there, with his head tucked under my chin.

"Is this only for this week?" he asks tentatively, the words slightly muffled against my shoulder.

"Do you want it to be? Because I'll be honest — Daddy/Boy relationships are more intimate to me. I usually get serious quickly. And because we live near each other back home, I can see us continuing and dating for real. But only if you want that. If you don't, we can have fun this week, you can trial what it's like to have a Daddy, and we can part ways as friends."

"You, um, last night, you...you called yourself my Daddy..." My heart stumbles a little, and I worry that I took things too far, too fast. But then he continues, "I liked the sound of that. I haven't had someone be mine in a long time." He's silent again for a moment, but I'm loath to push him, so I wait. Eventually, he starts again, "I...if this week goes well, I'd like to talk about how we can make it work back home, too. Because I haven't been as relaxed with anyone as I was last night in...in *ever*. I think...I think I need a Daddy. You. You as my Daddy."

I squeeze him closer, excited by the potential in his words. "So...we call this week a trial run? Like a taster of all the things we can offer each other?"

He nods. "Yeah. Yeah, I'd like that." Then he squirms and tentatively offers, "But, um, I think I need that change now...Daddy. Please."

My heart squeezes again at the sweet, cautious trial of the title on his tongue. It sounds good to hear him say it. Right.

"Good boy for asking so nicely," I tell him, nuzzling his head with my nose until I can pull back to look him in the eye. "Can I kiss you?"

"I have morning breath."

"So do I."

Rowan's full lips pull into another one of those shy smiles. "Then, yes, kiss me. Please...Daddy."

I do not need to be asked twice.

He tilts his head back and I dip forward, brushing my lips over his. I feel his breath hitch at the first touch of my mouth on his, and his fingers dig into the fabric of my t-shirt over my shoulder blades.

I press my lips against his more firmly, delighting in the way he melts in my hold, letting me guide and control the kiss. It's slow at first. Cautious, exploratory, building. As we get accustomed to the fit of each other's mouths, to the most comfortable angle of our heads, to the cadence of each other's breaths, it gets deeper. Our lips part, our tongues tentatively tease at each other, and our hips grind together until he whines and pulls back.

"Sorry," he looks away, "that can't feel good."

I cup his cheek. "What can't? Because I was feeling *very* good just now. Almost too good." I reach between us to push down on my throbbing cock, and he flinches away when I brush the front of his swollen diaper.

"That can't," he mutters.

"Oh, sweetheart." It's going to take more than one conversation to convince him that I really am more than okay with it. Still, the urge to hurt his previous boyfriends is strong. "Let's get you changed like I promised. Then we can talk about all the fun we're going to have today."

"Okay."

After confirming his traffic light color, I get him to lie back across the mattress like he did last night. I find wipes in his suitcase, along with his daytime diapers —which I affectionately think of as pull-ups— as well as a pair of swim trunk shorts and a t-shirt.

Like before, I talk Rowan through the steps of the change. He's more tense than he was last night, likely because he's used the diaper I'm removing, and because he's no longer on the cusp of sleep.

I kiss the inside of his thigh when I'm done wiping him clean, and I'm pleased to see a smile on his face when I reach for his pull-up.

"Gonna need you to stand up for the rest, baby," I tell him.

He nods, biting his lip when he sees the outfit I've selected. "I don't usually wear shorts," he admits after I've helped him step into each leg of his incontinence pants and pulled them up until they sat snugly around his waist. "I'm afraid people will notice..."

"Nobody will," I assure him. "But if you really hate the shorts, we can change to something looser, okay? However," I smile and wave the shorts at him, "you'll need these for swimming."

He blinks, jaw going slack. "Swimming? But...I can't wear this" —he points at his white, discreetly padded crotch— "in water."

"No. We'll take it off and go potty before we go swimming."

Rowan's handsome face contorts with anxiety. He doesn't even question my use of the 'p' word. Nibbling his lip, he says, "But...what if I go in the water? Sometimes I can last hours, but other times..."

"Then you pee in the pool or the ocean," I shrug. "If it's in the pool, the chemicals will take care of it." Besides, half the guys in this resort have probably released other fluids in the pool anyway, not that I say that out loud. "In the ocean, the constantly moving tide and the sheer volume of ocean water makes it a non-issue. Plus, where do you think all the fishies and things go to the bathroom, hmm?"

"That's different," he argues, but he's fighting a smile.

"How?"

"...I don't know, but it is."

I grin and kneel with the waistband of his shorts stretched out in invitation. "Come on, sweetheart. Now that I'm out of bed, I want breakfast."

Chapter Nine

We eat breakfast in the resort's restaurant, and are informed that it is, as the concierge promised yesterday, on the house. Like at dinner, Aaron and I chat easily about our interests —from our mutual preference of pineapple juice over orange juice, to deeper topics like the local charities we both support back home— and I can't help but think I must be in a coma or something.

Aaron is too perfect.

"So," he says, wiping the mouth I kissed earlier on his napkin, "the weather looks perfect for some time at the beach today. What do you think?"

The hotel's restaurant is located on the ground floor of the main building, right at the back. Like the place we ate last night, it has a deck that stretches out, overlooking the sand dunes of the beach and the rolling blue-green ocean beyond. We're sitting on the deck, the salty breeze ruffling our hair, and I sigh as I take in the pale blue, cloudless sky.

"It is a gorgeous day."

Aaron snorts. "You sound so disappointed by that."

Squirming in my seat, I shrug. "I'm not outdoorsy."

He reaches across the table and takes my hand, giving it a squeeze. "Is that out of choice? Or have you been limiting yourself because of your condition?"

"A bit of both, I think. I've been like this," I gesture vaguely over my body, "since I was nineteen. It's ingrained now."

He frowns. "Nineteen. That's rough."

"Yeah, well, I'm not dying from prostate cancer, so..."

Sitting back in his seat, Aaron issues a low whistle. "At *nineteen?*" he repeats. "That's so rare."

"I know. So were the complications from surgery. But lucky me, I got it all."

"I'm so sorry, Ro."

I wave him off. "Don't be. I'm alive, I'm otherwise fully functional. Things could be worse."

"That might be true, but you're still allowed to be upset about it. To acknowledge that it's still unfair."

Pushing the scraps of my meal around on my plate, I shoot him a little smile. "I appreciate that." Sitting back, I nudge my plate into the middle of the table. "Honestly, the incontinence wouldn't be as unbearable if I didn't also have to deal with the ED. That's what really ends up being the dealbreaker in most of my relationships. Men take it as an affront that I can't get hard for them, or on the off chance I do, when I come it's...kind of anticlimactic."

"I know you're not going to just take my word for it, but I'm not like that. I understand it from a medical perspective, which helps, but intimacy doesn't always have to be about sex, either."

He's so earnest as he says it, it makes my stomach flip-flop. "I still get enjoyment out of kissing and frotting and stuff, though. And making my boyfriends come, even if I can't get it up. But, in the end, most guys I've dated seem to think that they can 'fix' my ED by being good in bed, and when it doesn't happen..."

"They get frustrated, and their egos take a hit," he finishes for me, nodding. "Again, I know this sounds like lip service, but I'm confident in who I am as a lover and as a Daddy. It's not going to scare me off if I can't get you hard."

I really, *really* want to believe him. But he's right: I've heard that spiel before. Still, he's the first man to actively involve himself with my incontinence struggles, so maybe he'll be the first to genuinely understand my erectile dysfunction as well.

If he is a figment of a coma fantasy, he definitely will.

"So..." he prods as I try not to chuckle at my silly thoughts. "The beach?"

My stomach flips again, this time with nerves.

"What do you want to do at the beach?"

Aaron's pearly white teeth glint as he grins. "Well, we can hire all the equipment, right? So...what do you think of hiring a jet ski first, then maybe one of the kayaks?"

I bite my lip. "What if I need to *go*? I mean, while we're on the jet ski or kayak?"

"Pee in the ocean or the river," he says, like it's a simple solution. "We can even jump overboard to do it."

"We?"

"I'll pee in solidarity with you if it helps."

The flippant response startles a laugh out of me. None of my exes have ever been so casual about it. It's just one more thing that makes me feel like I'm going to get far too attached to him too soon. As if I'm not already.

"So, what do you say? Want to give some watersports a go?"

I arch an eyebrow, remembering what he said about his kinks yesterday. "Just so we're on the same page," I tease, "this time you *are* talking about snorkels and stuff?"

His smirk is devilish. "For now, baby. For now."

***

Being on a jet ski is actually a lot of fun. I cling to Aaron's red, neoprene life jacket, pressed up against his back as he drives the machine over the water. We bounce as we go over gentle ripples in the current, and I close my eyes, enjoying the wind and water spraying around us.

The sky above us is still clear of clouds, and the water around us is a deep, dark blue. I can't see more than a foot or two into it when we slow down, but it doesn't scare me like I thought it might. There are other boats and jet skis out on the water, but they are so far away that the people on them look like ants.

It's more peaceful and private than I thought it would be.

We've hired the jet ski for two hours, and the resort is now a speck on the horizon with how far we've traveled from the shore. Aaron slows down, then turns the engine off so we can take pictures of the coastline and of the straight blue line of the ocean where it meets the sky, stretching out into forever.

We rock gently as we sit and take it all in, and I'm starting to realize that this is the kind of thing I've been letting myself miss out on over the years. It's a bit sad to wonder what other kinds of fun I've deprived myself of.

"You okay, Ro?" Aaron asks as I fall quiet, my thoughts making my stomach churn unpleasantly.

Or is that my bladder twinging?

I'm kind of paranoid about that.

"Just…I don't know. Wondering how much I could have been doing all these years, I think," I confess quietly, painfully aware of the fact that I'm not wearing any kind of incontinence protection right now. It's just a pair of borrowed cotton underwear under my swim trunk shorts, which feels so strange after twenty-odd years of the disposable pants. I feel almost naked like this. Definitely exposed. Risky.

He half turns, craning his neck so he can look at me over his shoulder. His hair is wild from the wind and salty sea spray, and his cheeks are flushed from the same, and likely also from the sun. "Well, we're going to do as much as we can this week," he tells me decisively. "And, regardless of how the Daddy trial ends, when we get back home, we can hang out and do fun stuff together there, too. Even just as friends, if that's what you want."

I wish I could tell him that he can't make these promises. That *he* might be the one to realize that I'm too much effort with very little payoff. But the words get stuck in my throat and I just nod.

"I'd like that," I say, and it's not a lie.

I would like that.

Too much.

He smiles. "Me too."

We sit in silence for a few beats, and the water around us laps at the sides of the jet ski. It's a really relaxing sound…until it isn't.

All of a sudden, the urge to go strikes me, made more insistent by the wet lap-lap-lapping around us. I inhale sharply and try not to panic.

"What's wrong?" Aaron asks.

Releasing my hold on the handles on the sides of his lifejackets, I grip myself over my shorts. "I've…I've gotta…"

"Do you feel comfortable going over the side?" he asks calmly, scanning the horizon, presumably for any oncoming vessels. "Or do you want to get in the water and go?"

"But then I'll be all wet when I get back on the seat."

He shrugs. "They're waterproof, baby. They get wet from people doing tricks and stuff with them."

I squirm, feeling my body begin to make the decision for me. Really disliking the sensation of dampening cotton around my crotch, however light it might be, I scramble to my feet, turn, and jump off the back of the jet ski and into the cool ocean. The water around me soon warms at the same time as the skin on my cheeks does while I tread water, trying not to think about how scary it is being out in the middle of the ocean like this with no land for miles.

"That looked like fun," Aaron grins at me. "How's the water?"

I paddle awkwardly over to the back of the jet ski, hampered by the life jacket which is simultaneously making me feel super buoyant in the endless ocean. "It's a bit cool," I answer, "and I don't like the sticky, salty feeling on my skin."

"You prefer swimming in pools?"

"I haven't really swum since my teens, but...yeah."

There's a flicker of empathy in his dark eyes, but he nods. "I prefer pools, too."

It doesn't take me long to find the fold-down step at the rear of the machine, and I hoist myself back onto the seat with a little bit of effort. With how hot the sun is, I don't feel cold, despite being drenched from head to toe. I also feel liberated in a way I can't ever recall feeling.

"I can't believe I jumped into the ocean," I say as I get myself situated behind Aaron again, after checking that he doesn't mind me getting him all wet. "What if there are sharks out here?"

"Well, I feel like there might be," he answers, "but you weren't in there long enough for them to take a nibble."

I pause, my heart thumping. "Are you joking?"

"I mean, sharks live in the ocean, sweetheart. And Australia's kind of notorious for its deadly wildlife."

I look back into the dark depths and swallow. "Maybe next time I'll just pee over the side."

He chuckles before he presses the button to restart the engine.

Then we're off again, bouncing over little waves, and by the time we make it back to the resort, the wind and sun have mostly dried me off, and my cheeks hurt from smiling and laughing.

I can't ever recall feeling like this before.

I'm almost afraid that this really is a coma dream.

Chapter Ten

Aaron

Kayaking with Rowan is even more fun than riding the jet ski. There's a calm inlet on the far side of the resort, not really a full river or creek, but enough of a waterway for people to kayak, or hire the stand-up paddleboards and entertain themselves for a couple of hours. The water on this side of the resort is still and fairly clear; still deep, but nowhere near as fathomless as the ocean side.

Rowan still fusses about the possibility of sharks as we glide our paddles across the blue-green surface of the water, and I assure him that we will stick close enough to the shore that, if he should need to pee, he can leap off and sit in the shallows, safe from any lurking fins and teeth.

Despite his concerns, that makes him laugh. I've actually heard him laugh a lot today.

I get the feeling he doesn't laugh enough, usually.

If I have my way, he will laugh more often than not going forward.

"This kayaking thing isn't as easy as it looks," he mutters from behind me, pulling me out of my thoughts. "My arms aren't going to thank me after this."

I nod, my biceps straining as I dip my paddle down and effectively pull us forward in the calm water. "It's a fun workout," I reply, smiling to myself as he snorts.

"I think our definitions of 'fun' are different."

"Don't you write for a *lifestyle* magazine?" I challenge him. "Shouldn't that include enthusiasm for stuff like this? Picture-perfect scenery, blue skies, the sun—"

"Blaring down on us and increasing our risk of skin cancer?" Even though the words are dry and cynical, I can hear him smirking.

Sassy boy...

I turn my head to glance over my shoulder. "What do you write about, then?"

"I'm more of an editor now," he shrugs, then grimaces as he strains to paddle us forward against the current, "but *my* versions of heavenly retreats involve snifters of fine whiskey and crackling fireplaces. No manual labor involved." He makes another face as he raises the back of his hand to wipe at his sweaty forehead. "This just feels like—*ah!*" He leans sideways suddenly, rocking the whole kayak dangerously. "What the fuck was that?"

"What was what?" I peer over the right side of our vessel, which he is studiously avoiding.

"Well, if I knew, I wouldn't be asking."

I kind of like this snarky, bratty side of him. The more comfortable he's gotten with me, the more it has come out to play today. He's still a very sweet man, but after a couple of changes, I'm guessing he's slowly trusting that I'm not going to run away. Or maybe this is his way of pushing my boundaries. He's never been a Boy before, so I know at some point I will have to bring out the 'don't talk back to Daddy' rule.

Patiently, though, I ask, "What did it look like?"

"Like something moving in the water."

"Helpful."

He uses his paddle to scoop up some water and splash my lap.

"Hey!" I protest through spluttered laughter, "That was naughty, sweetheart."

"Yeah, well, you were mocking me."

"You were being vague."

"It was in the water, and it *moved*. Fast."

"Like...a fish?"

He's quiet for a second, then he laughs. "Shut up."

***

"Today was a lot of fun," I say, clasping Rowan's hand in mine and swinging it between us as we head back towards the main building. "Thank you for joining me."

"It was surprisingly fun," he agrees. "Jet skis and kayaks are things I never thought I'd try."

"And swimming in the middle of the ocean, don't forget that."

"Yeah, that's never happening again. Did you see that stingray go under the kayak on our way back? A *stingray*, Aaron." He shakes his head, bewildered.

I can't help teasing, "Who knew they lived in the wild?"

He stops and smacks at my bicep with an open palm. "Shut up. I just didn't expect to see one right near the resort."

"It was only a little baby ray." It really had been small, its body no larger than a dinner plate, and its barbed tail only a foot long, harmlessly swimming along in the shallows of the inlet. "I bet it would have been more scared of you than you are of it."

"That" —he turns and pokes his index finger into my chest— "is the Daddiest thing you've said all day." The pink of his cheeks, likely half-caused by overexposure to the sun, deepens, and he ducks his chin as he adds, "And you've changed me twice."

My lips curl into a bright smile. "You like it when I go all Daddy, though, don't you?"

"If I'm being honest...yeah. I do. I'm just..." We've made it back to the elevators and I press the 'up' triangle, waiting patiently for him to think before speaking. "It's going to take some time for me to get used to calling you...*that*."

Leaning against the wall, I reach for his hand and I squeeze it. "Sweetheart, it hasn't even been a full day yet. There aren't any rules on how quickly you need to get comfortable with saying or doing anything, inside kink or out of it. If you don't want to call me Daddy, that's okay, too."

He's silent as we step into the elevator, but as we step out onto our floor, he speaks again. "When I said it this morning, I liked it. When it was in our private space, it was easier to say it. But out where anyone could hear it..."

"Ro, I promise," I assure him as I swipe my keycard over the reader and let us into our room, "that's totally understandable. We'll do everything at your pace. I mean," taking him by the hand, I wander over to the couch and tug him down into my lap, sitting him sideways so I can look him in the eye, "because I'm Daddy and you're new to this, I'll make choices about new things I think you'll be comfortable with, but you can safe word out at any time. About anything at all. Even sitting in my lap right now. What's your traffic light color?"

"Green," he says without hesitation, wiggling his hips on my thighs. "It's nice to feel...I don't know...treasured, I guess."

Gently placing my hand on the back of his head, I pull him so his forehead is touching mine. "You deserve to be treasured, sweetheart."

Surprising me, Rowan twists around to straddle me fully, his knees sinking into the leather on either side of my hips. With his wrists looped behind my neck, he shyly asks, "Is this okay?"

"*Hmm,*" I pretend to think about it, making zero attempt to hide my smile, "hot Boy straddling my lap...is that okay? Gee, I'm not sure..." My smile only grows wider as he blushes and lets out a breathy little laugh. Settling my hands on his hips, I nuzzle my nose against his. "It's perfect, Ro."

He takes me by surprise again by initiating a kiss. There's nothing tentative about the meeting of our mouths this time around. He's confident as he slides his tongue between my lips, and I groan when he starts to rock his still-not-padded crotch against mine.

I lose myself in the slow, sultry movements of our mouths and of his body. My cock hardens and I feel his lips curving upwards, even while they're still sliding over mine.

"That's all you, baby," I tell him during a break for air.

He looks down, grins, then dives in to kiss me again before Rowan asks, "Think you could come from just this?"

"Keep grinding against me and that's a hell yes."

"Fuck, that's hot," he says before he leans in to kiss me again. His hips undulate faster, with more force, and I squeeze his ass, pulling him in closer, wanting to help him increase the friction.

It's not long before I'm teetering on the edge, but I'm not quite where I need to be. I have half a thought to ask him to reach between us and release my cock, but his breathing hitches as his body tenses.

"Baby," I pant as I pull out of the kiss, my hands still holding him in place, my eyes scanning his face while my scrambled brain tries to understand the sudden shift in his demeanor, "what—?"

He reaches between us to grip himself, his face contorting with discomfort and embarrassment. "I've gotta…"

Oh.

My cock throbs at the realization and I remind myself not to think with my dick.

I'm out of my usual routine, not having had a Boy in my life for a little while, and it shows.

I'm his Daddy. I should have thought about getting him changed back into his usual pull-up underwear or should have at least talked about the possibility of this happening before it got this far.

"You have a choice, baby," I hurry to tell him. "You can try to make it to the bathroom, and if you don't get all the way, there's nothing wrong with that. Or," I swallow, trying not to influence his decision by how badly I want him to choose this idea, "you can just let go. Now. Over my cock."

His eyes are wide, cheeks bright pink. He squirms in my lap, more a potty dance than the sexy movements from moments ago, but it still makes my dick jump and leak precum into my own underwear.

"There's no wrong choice, baby." I tell him as I watch the emotions cross over his face in rapid succession.

"I…you really want me to…"

"Traffic light?"

"Y-yellow," he squirms again, fingers tightening around his crotch while he snorts. "Kind of appropriate."

I want to talk through his concerns and his feelings, but I don't think we have enough time for that.

"I'm not going to judge you or shame you no matter what you choose to try, sweetheart," I tell him. "Daddy's got you either way. I'm sorry I didn't think ahead and that you're in this position because I didn't."

His hips rock against mine again and he shakes his head. "N-no. Don't be sorry. I...I should have thought ahead, too. I just got distracted."

"It's still your choice," I remind him. "We don't have to do this now."

Nodding, Rowan licks his lips and pulls his hand away from between us. "I trust you," he murmurs, making my heart flutter. Then he squeezes his eyes shut, his blush deepening as his lips part, and I feel it.

The rush of heat and wetness spreads over my cock and thighs as the pitter-patter sound of liquid hitting fabric competes with the sound of my heavy breathing and his quiet whimpers as he leans into me.

"Such a good boy," I croon into his ear, "let it all out. That's it, baby. Fuck that feels good." I grip his ass and gasp at the sensations of wet material and heat as I grind up into him. "I'm so —*nnngh*— proud of you, Ro."

Rowan buries his face in the crook of my neck, his breath coming in shallow pants. "D-daddy."

"Fuck, baby," I groan, my fingers digging into the supple globes of his ass. I grind into him shamelessly, chasing down the last spurts of his release.

"*Daddy*," he repeats again, sounding more certain about the word, almost like he's begging.

Combined with the sensory overload, the pleaded epithet and his warm breath against my skin is enough to send me over the edge. "Oh, god. *Rowan.* Sweetheart...*nnnngh.*"

My orgasm feels like it is wrenched from me, jets of cum adding to the mess that has become of my shorts and underwear. I'm wet and sticky, and it is all rapidly cooling with the air conditioner set to its most arctic setting. With my heart hammering, I feel filthy, but in the most satisfying way possible.

"Whoa," Ro breathes, sitting back to peer down at our laps. The fabric of our shorts clings to our skin, dark patches of moisture spreading over our thighs and down my hips. His cheeks are still red, and so are his eyes, but there's a shy smile tugging at his lips when he looks back up at my face. "You came."

Chuckling at the awe in his voice, I release his ass so I can cup his bearded jaw. I rub my thumb affectionately over the sharp salt and pepper hairs, relishing at the prickle and bite against my skin. "I wasn't lying when I said this is one of my kinks."

"No kidding." He looks down again. "Wow."

"I am still sorry that we didn't get to talk about it first. To plan it. I really should have thought about your potty schedule before—"

His snort cuts me off. "You really are a Daddy, aren't you? *Potty schedule,*" he repeats the words with a sardonic shake of his head. "I refuse to call it that, just so you know."

"Do you mind me using the word potty? Would you prefer 'bathroom'? It's just that last night you seemed to sink into some kind of headspace and, I won't lie, it's a habit for me. But if it makes you uncomfortable—"

"Daddy, it's fine. Who am I to stop you from using a word that makes you happy?" Rowan seems remarkably composed and calm, given the situation. I was expecting him to panic about it.

To be more upset, especially when we accidentally found ourselves like this without proper negotiation. He looks down between us again and scrunches his nose. "And I *am* fighting some kind of headspace right now, I think. Like...having an accident makes me feel really" —he rolls his neck— "young and vulnerable, I guess? Small? Needy? I don't know. A bit of all of it. I'm not used to letting other people see me that way. Or like this." He waves his hand over his crotch. "But you really do enjoy all of this. I mean, you...you *came*. I...I've never...This is supposed to feel shameful. I'm not supposed to enjoy it."

My face pulls into a scowl before I can control my reaction, and he laughs wetly, shaking his head again before he presses his forehead to mine.

"I know you disagree with me. It's just going to take some time for me to work through twenty years of different experiences to this one." He sighs, then pulls back again, cringing, "But, um, could we go clean up now?"

Smiling warmly, I nod and lean forward to kiss his lips softly and sweetly. "Of course, sweetheart. Want to shower with Daddy?"

Chapter Eleven

Despite fighting the strange, floaty feeling in my head, and the urge to hand over control to what feels like a younger, more helpless version of myself, I allow myself to think of Aaron as Daddy as he helps me off his lap and into the bathroom. He undresses me with the same kind of gentle reverence as when he diapered me, tossing my soiled pants and underwear into a pile in the corner of the bathroom, then lobbing my shirt on top.

His clothes follow more hastily, and I realize that this is the first time I'm seeing him naked. He's just as gorgeous out of his clothes as in them. With a smooth, hairless chest (completely different to my furry one), a lean abdomen, and surprisingly muscular thighs considering the rest of his build, he's perfection. Even his cock looks perfect, nestled in a thatch of trimmed dark pubic hair currently matted with the evidence of how much he enjoyed...well, the *thing* that happened on the couch.

Jesus, I...I peed on him. And he liked it.

And I *liked* that he liked it.

I want to do it all again.

Twenty-odd years of experience tells me that I should be disgusted by those particular inclinations. But a couple of minutes on the couch with Aaron says otherwise.

He came.

He came hard. Calling my name.

After I urinated all over his lap.

And he wasn't ashamed of that. He wasn't embarrassed that we were sitting in a puddle of my pee, and he really didn't seem at all bothered by me knowing how much he enjoyed the whole thing. And, for a brief moment, I felt good. Proud, even.

I had done that. *I* made him come in his underwear. *Me.*

But those feelings conflict with everything any of my exes have ever said about my lack of bladder control.

It feels selfish to have liked that so much. Selfish and weird and wrong.

Dirty.

"Do you want to talk about it now, or after the shower?" Aaron asks, taking my hand and squeezing it. "Because your thoughts are written all over your face, Ro. Which is why I am sorry we didn't get to plan that. That you didn't get much of a choice about if you really wanted to do that or not. About if you were ready."

"I liked it," I blurt, feeling my cheeks burn with the confession. "I didn't expect to like it. And everything I've ever thought about my condition and...and my accidents..."

"I know, sweetheart. It's confronting. But," he squeezes my hand, waiting until I meet his gaze before he smiles, "there's nothing wrong with enjoying yourself. It was consensual. You know I liked it." He sweeps a hand over his crotch, his smile turning crooked. "And it was private. Nobody else ever needs to know what we do together if you don't want them to. The only people who need to be okay with any of it are us. Just you and me."

His words calm my inner turmoil. He's right. My shame and embarrassment comes from what other people have thought and have said. Other people who have hurt me and left me. Their thoughts and opinions stopped mattering years ago, so why should I be concerned about any of that now? Especially when, for the first time I can recall, my issues don't feel like a roadblock. If anything, they feel like something Aaron and I can turn into positives between us.

It was one thing to know, hypothetically, that Aaron wouldn't freak out if one of my nightmare scenarios played out in real time. But to see his acceptance —his *enjoyment*— in action? It's too good to be true.

I am actually glad that we didn't plan it. That I got to see his genuine reaction to something happening in the moment. That none of it felt rehearsed or premeditated or negotiated.

Aaron's hand is warm and solid in mine, anchoring me to the here and now.

Am I okay with what we did? What we'll continue doing? The diapers and the golden showers and whatever else we try?

My heart thumps wildly with nervous anticipation.

I am.

***

Later, after the shower (where Daddy washed me with a tenderness that almost brought tears to my eyes), dressing, and cleaning up the couch, we sit on the lanai and look out over the lush greenery that stretches towards the oceanside. We're both sipping mimosas, and I'm not worried about the wine going through me.

Instead, we talk about how much fun we had on the water today, about maybe visiting Australia Zoo (which is only an hour or so south of our resort), and about other places we might like to explore while we're here.

Eventually, the conversation turns back to what happened on the couch. I appreciate that Aaron has given me time to process it all properly, but I'm not freaking out. I made my choice; it turned out to be the right one, and I tell him so.

"I just worry that my lack of foresight took away your consent," he says, turning away from the pretty view to look me in the eye. He's completely serious, and my heart sinks to think that he's been worrying about this for the past couple of hours while I have been reveling in how amazing it was.

I reach for his hand and squeeze it. "You did give me a choice," I remind him. "Sure, in an ideal world, we might have planned it all out, but I think I'm starting to like being impulsive when it comes to you."

His lips quirk and his fingers tighten around mine. "Yeah?"

"Yeah."

Ever since the moment he sauntered up to the reception desk and rescued me, I've been impulsive with Dr. Aaron Park. And every snap decision so far has led to good things. Except for almost being shark food. Hard pass on that happening again.

"And...you did enjoy it? Your first watersports experience?"

I could have shuffled off his lap and I might have even had enough time to make it to the bathroom before disaster struck, but I chose to stay and share my loss of control with him.

I reflect on the relief of letting go, and on how secure I felt in his lap, and how surprised I was to feel his cock swelling and twitching through an orgasm. For the first time ever, I made the choice to piss myself and, for the first time ever, I liked the results.

I liked the way Aaron's fingers had dug into my ass. I liked his blissed-out moans and panted-out encouragement. I loved hearing my name spill from his lips as he reached the ultimate peak of pleasure.

I felt like I was in control of that.

"I really did," I answer honestly. "It...it took something I've been ashamed of for so long and has given me a positive memory. Something to look back on and say 'it doesn't have to be disgusting, it can be hot'. And watching you come made it hot. It made me feel sexy in a way I've never felt sexy before."

It's hard to describe the feeling, because wetting myself also brought on that sensation of being small, too, even while I felt empowered sexually.

Aaron's smile is filled with understanding, and he nods. "To me, it is *so* sexy. I feel genuinely privileged that you trusted me to be so vulnerable. I don't take that trust lightly, sweetheart."

"I know. Everything you have done so far has proven that far more than words alone possibly could." Shaking my head, I look over the trees again, catching a glimpse of the ocean glinting gold and orange with the fading sun. "It's hard to believe I've only known you a couple of days. It already feels like we've known each other for years."

Hell, I'm closer to Aaron than I ever was with Alex or the men I dated before him. I've done things with him I never would have imagined doing with Alex, even if Alex had asked me to. Is this what he meant when he said that BDSM relationships feel more intimate much sooner? It must be.

"I feel that way, too," he tells me. "We have so much more to learn about each other, but I'm already hoping that we can continue dating when we go home. That we can make a real relationship work between us."

Any remaining tension or fear that I'm allowing myself to get too attached too soon evaporates at his words. I'm learning quickly that I can take whatever he says at face value, and the fact that he wants the same things that I do lifts a weight from my shoulders. It makes my next words come easily and naturally, as if I was born to say them.

"I hope we can, too, Daddy."

Chapter Twelve

Aaron

After spending two more days together, exploring the resort and the Sunshine Coast together, it really does feel like Rowan and I have been together forever. After that first —mildly accidental— foray into watersports, something seems to have clicked for him. Diaper changes are green lit without hesitation or embarrassment, the Daddy title falling from his lips readily when we are alone. He asks me to make decisions for him, from choosing his outfits and his meals to deciding our itineraries for the day, and the genuine joy that radiates from him as we wander down the beach or through the resort hand-in-hand seems incongruous with the anxious, defeated Rowan I met only a few days ago.

It was obvious to me that he was touch-starved, so I've made a point to always reach out to him in some capacity whenever the opportunity allows. I hold his hand, or place mine on the base of his spine, or sling an arm around him wherever we go. He huddles close when we're in public, and prefers to sit in my lap when we're in private. In bed, he complains if we're not spooned together, relying on the air conditioning to get rid of the sticky Australian summer heat from our skin.

We talk through every new experience —whether it be kink-related or not— and I'm constantly wondering how anyone could have let him go, because he is one of the sweetest men I've ever met.

I know that I'm seeing Vacation Rowan right now, though, just like he's seeing Vacation Aaron. We're relaxed, neither of us encumbered by the stresses and pressures of our lives back home.

Will things change when we do go home? Most likely.

We will need to work out a schedule around my shiftwork. We will need to see how he feels about the Daddy/Boy dynamic sliding into his real life; whether he can be a Boy in between his job as the Editor In Charge of a magazine. Whether he's still comfortable letting go and letting me change him when we're back in the city where he's used to being so independent.

At this point, though, I am completely smitten. If we get home and being a Boy while managing his day-to-day life is too hard for Rowan, that's okay with me. I'm falling for him as a man and partner, not just for how compatible he is for my kinkier side. Like I told him at the start: it's all about balance and making sure he's happy. That's what will make me happy, too.

But wow is it weird to feel so intensely about him so soon. Not just because of the kink, but because he is everything I've wanted in a partner. Intelligent, kind, communicative, sweet...he ticks all of those boxes and then some. We like the same foods, happily watch the same kind of TV shows, and even though he was adamant that he was a homebody, Rowan has been just as interested in exploring during this vacation as I am.

We seem compatible in so many ways, and I am becoming increasingly invested in seeing him discover himself, too.

And that's what he's doing. Now that he's not as afraid of having to hide his condition, or of having to compensate for it, he's living life outside of the confines of the nearest bathroom. His confidence in himself seems to be growing by the minute, and it fills me with pride.

"Daddy," he murmurs, checking over his shoulders to make sure we're alone on our beach walk, "can we go back to the room?"

The sand between my toes is gritty and clinging to me, seeing as we are walking barefoot along the hard packed sand where the waves are drifting in over our skin, having broken a handful of feet away and carried forward with the momentum of the tide. The water slowly leeches back to whence it came, only to repeat the process again and again, with a dull roaring sound with every rush and crash of a wave. I find it relaxing in the blazing heat of the afternoon, living for the sea breezes accompanying the waves.

"Sure, baby. Getting too hot?"

Rowan's skin is a mild pink color, even though we have been applying sunscreen religiously. Sweat rolls down his temples and gathers at the roots of his salt and pepper streaked hair. He bites his lip and nods.

"And I need a change."

He's gotten so good about asking when he needs help, about not squirming away in embarrassment when his body does what it is wont to do. The lack of shame now seems miles apart from the panicked man in that restaurant bathroom stall.

It's mindboggling to think that it has only been three days, but I'm not naïve enough to believe it will always be this easy for him. Returning to his real life is going to be a challenge.

I squeeze his hand and smile. "Good boy," I praise, delighting in the way he fights a pleased, coy little smile, "thank you for telling me."

We turn on the spot and meander back over the sand, discussing dinner plans along the way. Proving that he's in tune with my own thought process, Rowan eventually asks, "Do you think it will feel this easy when we're back home?"

"Probably not," I answer honestly. "Not with having to work around our jobs. But," I hasten to add, "I think our dynamic is pretty solid."

"Me too," he admits, then scrunches his nose. "I'm kind of used to not panicking about" —a vague gesture encompasses his crotch area— "y'know. Even just knowing that you'll help get me all cleaned up and...well, I won't have that once I'm back in the office. It will be back to setting myself alarms and watching my fluid intake and making sure I have spare clothing on hand."

The words are accompanied by a sigh, and the echoes of the exhaustion and resignation that were etched into him the day we met.

"I know, sweetheart, and I'm sorry. But when we're both off work, we'll have *this*." I squeeze his hand, referencing our relationship. "And we'll make sure we get into a routine that works for us."

"Except...well, you're talking like you want to spend every waking moment of your free time outside of work with me," Rowan looks out over the rolling ocean, his gaze going distant. "That doesn't seem healthy. Or fair. You've got a social life, too, I'm sure."

"Not much of one at the moment," I admit. "I haven't lived in the city long. I only transferred a couple of months ago and I've mostly been working. There's a community center I was planning on checking out, though. It caters to people in the BDSM lifestyle, and I was thinking I might go to one of their social events to make some likeminded friends, you know?" I give his hand another squeeze as we turn to head up the sloping dunes towards the resort, our feet slipping in the soft sand as we work our legs to get up the gentle hill. "If you were comfortable joining me, maybe we could make some friends in the lifestyle together. Eventually, I mean. I know this is all still new to you."

He's quiet as he processes, panting against the physical activity of trudging through the sand, but once we've reached the path that leads back to the resort, he says, "People like us? Like…" in the periphery of my vision, his Adam's apple bobs, "like me?"

"People exploring ABDL?" I confirm and he nods. "Yeah, exactly. And other people in the age play and BDSM community, and people who have kinks or are in relationships which aren't considered 'standard' by society." I wait a moment before repeating, "But it's not something you need to decide right now. Maybe we can talk about it in a few months' time? And if you'd prefer to keep our dynamic purely private, that's okay, too."

He nods again. "I'll think about it."

"There's no rush to make any of these decisions, baby. I'm not going anywhere."

And I'm not. He's too precious to let go of.

Maybe one day he will believe that of himself, too.

Chapter Thirteen

Waking up on our last full day of vacation brings a bittersweet feeling with it. The last week has felt like something out of a dream. I never could have imagined that I'd feel comfortable wearing shorts or putting myself in situations where bathrooms weren't readily accessible, that I would find a companion who doesn't get grossed out when my bladder lets go without my permission and who isn't embarrassed when it happens in public, but all of that has been true.

I've even rediscovered a love of swimming —in pools, not the ocean— which the me of a week ago would have scoffed at. But here I am.

And, as if to punctuate just how dreamlike this whole thing is, I've woken up hard, my cock straining against the damp confines of my nighttime diaper.

Aaron has been amazing about my ED to this point. We've fooled around, grinding together in bed and on the couch, and with me giving him a couple of blowjobs in the shower, and he's never once sulked that I haven't physically gotten off with him, despite how much I have enjoyed our time together. But I can't lie and say I haven't wished that I could get it up for him, that I could experience an orgasm with him, because I have.

And now there's a chance that I can, assuming this surprise erection doesn't deflate as unexpectedly as it appeared.

"Daddy..." I croon, rocking my hips against his side, feeling a bit naughty for enjoying the press of squishy, moist cotton against my hard cock. I feel bubbly and light inside as I playfully tease, "My diaper needs attention."

Aaron snorts and cracks an eye open, turning his head to smile at me, curiosity dancing in his dark eyes. "That's a new one."

You're about to discover how new.

I squirm and affect a pout, trying to ignore the little jolts of pleasure from my movement. They're familiar, but also like a long-lost memory, the kind of sensation I wish I could experience more often, but I know that if I indulge too much now, I'll come too soon. I want to extend this for as long as my body will allow. "*Please*, Daddy?"

"It's unfair that it has taken you less than a week to work out my kryptonite," he grumbles, but he's smiling as he presses a kiss to my forehead and then rolls out of the bed to grab the wipes and a pair of my daytime protection underwear. Little does he know, he won't be needing the latter just yet.

I get into position for him, unable to hide my smirk as he carefully undoes the tabs of my diaper, rolling the sodden cotton and plastic away with his usual reverence.

"Well, I see why we were so insistent this morning," he says as my cock springs up to say hello, and there's equal parts warmth and arousal in his gaze and he looks up to meet mine. "How are you feeling about this, baby?"

"Pretty fucking ecstatic, actually," I answer honestly. "It's been a while." An embarrassingly long while since I was hard with a partner, actually, not that I say as much out loud. Of course, I remember how important consent is to Aaron, and then I feel guilty that I have literally just sprung my hard dick in his face and—

"I'm so happy you want to share this with me," he says, interrupting my thought spiral and unknowingly easing my concerns. "I'm still going to wipe you down, though, okay?"

My cock twitches enthusiastically at the idea of any sort of contact and I blush. "Yes please, Daddy."

He works quickly with the wipes, cleaning off my skin before disappearing into the bathroom to get rid of the trash and wash his hands. When he returns, he sets a bottle of lube on the nightstand, undresses, and then climbs into bed beside me, seizing my mouth with a firm, glorious kiss. My cock dribbles precum at that alone, and I gasp into Aaron's mouth when his hand wraps around my length and strokes, spreading the stickiness over my hardened flesh.

"This okay?" he asks.

Already breathless and overwhelmed by how amazing it is to be touched by someone else like this again, I can only nod.

We kiss some more, tongues sliding languidly over each other, before he pulls back again to ask, "How do you want this morning to play out, sweetheart? You're running the show right now."

My heart hammers with arousal and adrenaline. I want it all. I want him to jerk me off. I want to rut my cock against his. I want to roll him onto his back and fuck him. I want him to ride me. I want to feel his mouth on me, to spill into the perfect wet, warm suction my tongue has experienced.

Logically, I know this isn't going to be the only erection I ever experience with him. But it's my first, and I want everything with him.

Clearly sensing my indecision, he strokes me slowly and soothes, "I'm gonna love it all, Ro. Close your eyes...that's it...now tell me, what do you see yourself doing with this perfect cock today? No limits, baby."

My unlimited options race through my head, inspiring visuals that have me on the edge of release without actually doing any of them. "In—" I gasp and roll my hips, "Inside you. I want...I want to be inside you."

"Good boy," his praise does nothing to settle the bubbling euphoria and pleasure of the moment, nor does the new kiss he draws me into; this one hotter and needier than the previous ones. Then, blissfully, he takes over, tugging my shirt over my head, leaving us both naked.

"On your back, sweetheart. Daddy's going to ride you."

I scramble to obey while he grabs the bottle of lube. "I'm on PrEP and get tested regularly for work. My test last month was negative, and I haven't gone bare since my breakup two months ago. But I have condoms in my bag if you want—"

I'm shaking my head before he can even finish speaking. "I'm on PrEP, too. I haven't been with anyone in over a year. My annual physical was six months ago, and I tested negative then."

"So, you're good with going bare?" He double checks. "Color?"

"Green. So green I'm practically Kermit the frog."

"*Ohhh*, we're bringing puppets into the bedroom. I *knew* you had surprise kinks, baby."

"He's a Muppet not a puppet," I correct while laughing. "Now shut up and kiss me."

He complies with my demand, but not before cheekily asking, "Excuse me, but which one of us is the Daddy?"

I don't get to reply, though, because I'm swept up into the kiss, and then he's pressing the lube into my hands and I'm too distracted by the process of opening him up while he straddles me. It's been a really long time since I last topped, because Alex didn't bottom, but muscle memory takes over and I relish the feeling of sinking my slicked up fingers inside Aaron's willing body, where he is warm and tight and perfect. I tear my mouth away from his to watch his facial expressions as he bounces on my digits, moaning when I crook my fingers and graze his sweet spot.

"Oh, *yes*, baby," he arches his back, "more of that."

Supported by pillows against the headboard, I reach for his neglected cock with my free hand, trying not to come at the sensory overload of his hand on my dick, and mine both on him and inside him while he continues to make decadent sounds of pleasure.

"Fuck," he groans after a few more moments of scissoring my fingers while he rides them, "Ro, that feels too good. Need you in me now."

I'm enjoying myself too much, too, but the hint of Daddy voice in his demand has me pulling my fingers out and grappling blindly for the lube bottle again. It's funny how I've already been conditioned to respond to that voice, to that hint of dominance laced with affection. Maybe I was always made to be someone's sub. Someone's Boy.

No, not someone's. Aaron's.

I've never been one to really believe in fate or destiny or anything particularly airy-fairy, but I have no other way to justify all the coincidences that brought us together. It honestly feels like it was meant to be.

And, once my cock is slicked up and he's lowering his body down onto me, that feeling solidifies in my chest.

Because *fuck* he feels amazing.

"Y-you good?" he pants once he's fully seated. I blink up at him, bewildered.

"Shouldn't I be asking you that?"

His lips quirk. "Daddy habits die hard...*nnngh*. Fuck, baby, your cock is filling me up so good." He's rolling his hips slowly, setting the pace while I flounder underneath him.

I can't decide where to put my hands or how to get my mouth on some part of him — *any* part of him. He's so tight around my cock, warm and slick from the lube, and it's taking all my concentration not to come too soon.

"*Daddy*," I whine, and I can't even be embarrassed by the sound as it leaves my lips, "you feel amazing. I'm already close."

He groans and increases his pace, leaning forward to kiss me, his hips still undulating. "Hold it for me, Ro. Don't come yet."

Oh god.

The command is hot and terrifying all at once, because the sheer pleasure I get from being ordered not to come is making all my synapses fire up.

"*Daddy...*" I gasp against his lips, my body bouncing with his movement on top of me.

"Be a —*oh*, Jesus— be a good boy, Rowan."

Fuck. Fuck. Fuck. Fuck.

Each unspoken curse matches with a thrust of my hips into him, with a landing of his firm, youthful ass against my bare skin.

My balls draw up almost painfully tight. After so long without a partner, and literal years of not topping, I'm beyond overwhelmed by the pleasure of this connection.

"D-Daddy..." I can't vocalize anything else. Just a plaintive repetition of the special title I use for him in private. The one that symbolizes how different he is to every other man I've been with. The one that highlights my trust in him. My brain feels like soup. Floaty, bubbly, near-orgasming soup. "Daddy, I can't..."

"You *can*," he insists, sitting back up and bouncing so hard that the headboard rhythmically thumps against the wall. He enunciates through exhalations with every drop down onto my cock. "You. Can. Hold. It."

Why is it such a fucking turn on to be denied like this?

My hands —which had settled on his hips without my conscious decision— grip him tightly. I'm afraid that I'll leave bruises, but then the thought of leaving my marks on him makes my body tremble on the edge of what feels like unpreventable release.

"*Daddy!*" I cry, not wanting to disappoint him, but unable to be his good boy for much longer. "I'm gonna come."

He grabs for one of my hands and directs it to where his dick is flushed red and leaking onto my belly. He wraps my fingers around the shaft, closing his fist over mine, guiding me with the pressure and pace he needs. "Touch me, Rowan. Touch my cock. Make me come with you."

I can't even count the strokes. I'm too busy trying not to give in to my body's desperate urges.

"*Yes,*" he encourages on his next hard landing in my lap, the word more a growl than an actual word, "that's it. Good boy. I'm close, baby. So close."

I can't reply, any words I might have said now reduced to a garbled whine at the back of my throat as I finally lose control. "*Uuuuungh,*" I scramble to explain, "I'm c-coming—*ah!*—Daddy."

Alex always said my orgasms are a bit lacklustre. I guess they feel more intense for me than the amount of cum I produce would lead anyone to believe. But that doesn't bother me, and especially not today. Not with Aaron's body tensing as his own release hits him, ropes of his cum jetting out over my shuttling fist and onto my bare belly. We shudder and roll through the last moments of mutual bliss, before I start to soften and slip out of him, much to my disappointment.

Aaron climbs off me and collapses at my side, pressing sloppy, lazy kisses over my shoulder while he catches his breath.

"Mmm," he practically purrs as he spoons my side, seemingly unbothered by the mess on my belly or inside him, "you can wake me up for that anytime, Ro."

I snort. "It's practically a once-in-a-blue-moon event, so…maybe in another six months?" I'm exaggerating, but it really does feel that way sometimes. My body is unpredictable, and in moments like this it is hard not to resent my circumstances, but when Aaron just presses more kisses to my skin and tells me there's no pressure, the bitterness fades away, and I melt back into enjoying the afterglow again.

***

We spend the last day of our vacations exploring other parts of the Sunshine Coast, having Googled together over the course of the week. Our morning is spent in a place called Montville, out in the hinterland.

Much like Noosa, the tourist strip is a street filled with boutique stores —everything from fudge confectioners to clothing and souvenirs— and restaurants and cafes. It has a quaint vibe, like it is trying to feel as though it has simultaneously stepped back in time and is also meeting the demand for things to be sleek and modern. The buildings clash in terms of architectural design, some cottages and some all glass and white surfaces, but it is pretty and surrounded by lush greenery and, on one side of the street, epic views of the coastline peeking through behind leafy trees.

We spend a couple of hours meandering through the boutique stores and taking photos of the view. It's not quite as hot up here as down on the beachfront, but it's still warm and humid. Daddy makes sure that I stay hydrated, and my momentary freakout about the potential ramifications —about not finding a bathroom, or of wetting myself in such a crowded environment— is snuffed the second he takes my hand and squeezes it.

He doesn't even need to say anything to remind me that I'm not alone and that nobody else will know if I have an accident. My panic recedes as if by magic, and his confidence and acceptance seems to melt into me as if by osmosis.

"Good boy," he praises lowly, at a volume only meant for my ears. The words make me feel effervescent inside, much like they did the first time he said them. I don't think my body's response to them will ever change.

"Where to next?" I ask him after we've explored most of the street. My t-shirt is clinging to my skin, and I'd honestly like to do something in air-conditioning, or go back to the resort for one last dip in the pool.

Thankfully, Daddy seems to be on the same wavelength. "I think we should go back to the resort. I've booked a sunset cruise along the river for tonight, so why don't we chill this afternoon so we're refreshed for our last night here?"

It sounds perfect, but I can't help the pang of melancholy that strikes deep in my solar plexus at the words 'our last night here'.

This whole vacation has been something out of a dream. I'm still not convinced that I'm not comatose in a hospital somewhere, allowing my imagination to build a fantasy future to cope with whatever trauma landed me there.

I know things will be different when we're back home. I'll be back to my lonely apartment, for one thing. No more waking up snuggled against Aaron's warm body, strangely looking forward to him changing me out of my wet nighttime diaper, his gentle touch and sweet reverence something I have already become addicted to. No; instead, I'll wake up most mornings cold, damp and alone. Sad and resentful of my condition.

Our time together will need to be scheduled, too. Around my long workdays and his rotating shift work. Not to mention our individual social lives. I mean, sure, I really only ever hang out with Bianca, but I know Aaron has friends of his own, too. We won't be in our own special bubble anymore, and I can't help but worry that he won't enjoy me as much when things are more difficult. Especially when there are apparently kinky clubs and community centers filled with people who are probably a much better fit for him than me.

And that's the crux of my real worry: right now, I'm convenient. But back home, he could find a Boy —a Little— that meets all of his kinky needs, not just the diaper play. Because I still haven't allowed myself to sink into any kind of regression around him. The idea of dressing or sounding like a baby or toddler just isn't for me, even if some part of me is tempted to give in and see where those floaty, youthful urges take me.

Aaron said I might be more Middle than Little, which I've Googled this week, too. But that left me feeling more confused than ever, because Middles aren't usually associated with diaper play and...well. I just don't think I fit anywhere, not even in his kinky community.

Even so, I'm selfish, and I don't want to lose him. Not after such a magical week together. Not after the way he's been able to make me feel normal for the first time in my adult life. Like a partner and not a burden.

"Baby, where did you go?" Aaron guides me to a park bench in a small leisure area dominated by shady trees. He sits me down and lifts my chin, gently forcing me to meet his worried gaze. "Are you okay?"

"It's the end of vacation blues, I think," I tell him half the truth, not sure how to express my fears that I won't be enough for him once we're back home. "This trip has been amazing" —I take a deep breath— "because of you."

Understanding seems to dawn on him. "Sweetheart..."

"I would probably have spent the week hiding in my resort room," I continue on with a shake of my head, "if you hadn't made me feel like all this is okay." I wave my hand over my lower body, then sigh. "I've been on a jet ski, and a kayak, and I swam in the ocean. I petted kangaroos and koalas at the zoo. I even went on a hike to that waterfall, even though I knew there were *no* bathrooms for that...and I never would have done any of it without knowing you were there to help me if my body failed me."

"It doesn't fail you, Ro. It just works differently to other peoples' bodies."

I shrug, not bothering to tell him that he's the first man to ever think that way about my incontinence. He knows he is. "That's just it," I say instead, "you've made me feel...I don't know...*better* in my own skin. Safer in public. And now..."

"Now we're going home, and I can't be there all the time."

"I'm forty-one," the words are bitter and full of self-deprecation. "I shouldn't need another man to hold my hand twenty-four-seven."

"There's nothing wrong with wanting or needing support, Ro. In my fantasies, there's nothing I want more than to be your Daddy full-time. To not have to worry about work and just...be together. Like we have been this week."

"Even though I don't do the age play stuff?" The insecure question tumbles from my lips before my filter can contain it, and I cringe.

He's quiet for a moment, his dark eyes assessing me before he says, "You're still worried that you're not enough for me. That our dynamic is lacking."

I shrug again, looking away. Sunlight filters through the trees above us, making pretty gold patterns on the dark green grass at our feet. A light breeze makes the patterns dance.

"Honey, you might not realize it, but you do regress with me. You're doing it now."

That makes me startle. "What?"

His expression softens and he pulls my hand into his lap, holding it tightly between both his warm palms. "When you relax, you definitely seem to slip into a more...I guess juvenile...headspace. It's why I said I think you're more Middle than Little. Are you into stuffies and sippy cups and pacifiers? No. But you do seem younger. Innocent. Sweet and a bit pouty," he grins and bumps my shoulder with his. "Like a hurting teenager, I guess. I haven't pushed you to explore it, though, because this is all new for you, and because we've been getting to know and trust each other. But," he gives my hand a little tug and shake, "whether you regress further or not, you're perfect as you are, Rowan. I'm falling for every single facet of you."

Swallowing hard, and ignoring the suddenly rapidly beating of my heart, I ask, "But...what if you meet someone at the community center or at that BDSM club you mentioned? Someone more experienced with the lifestyle and regressing?"

He shakes his head, then pulls me in for a hug. His heart feels like it is beating just as quickly as mine. "I don't want anyone else," his voice rumbles through his chest as he speaks. "Being with you is everything I've been looking for, Ro. I'm falling for you."

So I didn't imagine it before. And it wasn't a slip of the tongue.

Choked up, I bury my face in the crook of his neck. "I'm falling for you, too, Aaron." Pausing, I lick my lips, then correct myself, "Daddy."

Chapter Fourteen

Our final night feels heavier than I thought it would. After our unexpected conversation in the morning, we came back to the resort and spent the afternoon cuddling and languorously making out, holding on tightly to each other.

Rowan's insecurities will take a lot longer than a week to work through, but it still hurts my heart to know that he's so worried things will fall apart once we get back home.

But those concerns are pushed aside when it is time to leave for our sunset cruise up the river. I worried yesterday when I booked our spots, because the weather had turned and we experienced one of Queensland's famed summer thunderstorms from our hotel room, but today the weather has been picture perfect and the sky has been clear.

The boat we board is gleaming white and modern, with an open deck and a small cash bar. Five other couples join us, and we all mingle and make small-talk before the captain gives us a mandatory safety talk and then departs from the dock.

It's almost a lazy meander down the river, and we all peel off into our private bubbles, scattered around the deck. An elderly couple takes two of the seats facing the helm, content to drink in the sights more comfortably than standing. Rowan walks to the handrail, just off-center from the bow, and leans against the railing, and I bracket him in from behind, resting my chin on his upper back. It might look silly, the shorter of us being the big spoon, but the way he melts every time I take up this position makes it perfect.

In front of us, the sky is turning orange and pink, with a few scattered, fluffy clouds almost appearing purple from the backlighting. The dark, still water of the river glints with the light show above us, reflecting back the golds and purples and pinks from the sky. It's beautiful, and the murmur of low voices fades away while everyone on board just absorbs the moment.

"Want to take a selfie?" I ask Rowan, barely speaking above a whisper.

He nods, his hair ruffled from the slight breeze, enhanced as it is by the slow push of the boat through the water. I step back and he turns to face me, then I turn my back and press into him, holding up my phone with the front-facing camera enabled. I angle it and we smile, trying to capture the splendor of the backdrop behind us in all its glory.

But when I look at the final shots, it's not the rainbow of color at our backs which catches my breath. It's the adoration on Rowan's face.

***

"I can't believe you upgraded me to Business Class," Rowan mutters as we settle ourselves into the plush plane seats. "I've never flown Business in my life."

"I wanted my Boy to sit with me," I shrug. "And I very rarely travel, so why not do it in comfort if I can afford it?"

We've not really spoken about our financial situations, but I grew up privileged. Both of my parents were extremely successful doctors before their retirement —my father, Kim Park, a cardiologist, and my mother, Elizabeth Whitman-Park, a neurosurgeon— and I grew up with all the perks you might imagine that entails. Private schools, extracurriculars, somewhat extravagant summer childhood vacations: the works. I'm a trust fund baby, and I am aware that I am extremely lucky for my lot in life.

My father instilled that in me from a young age, having come to the United States from Korea with nothing but a medical degree under his belt. He worked hard to attain the ability to practice in the USA, then built his entire career from the ground up. He met my mother early in his career, at the first hospital where he worked, and he promised her that he would work hard to give her the life he believed she deserved. Being the feminist that she is, Mom told him they'd do it together.

Forty-five years, four children, and a lot of successful investments later, and they are the kind of couple I want to emulate. Happy, in love, and not afraid to work hard to achieve their goals together. But their story also reminds me not to take my position in life for granted. If they hadn't worked as hard as they did, my life could have looked very different. So I don't splash my cash often —I don't drive an insanely expensive car or live in a lavish penthouse, not that there's anything wrong for those that can afford to and who find joy in it— but when I do splurge, it's on experiences that make me and the people I love happy.

And, while I know that Rowan isn't struggling financially, I know that he's not the kind of man to spend money on Business Class tickets, even if they are far more comfortable for a flight duration of over thirteen hours.

He shakes his head, his cheeks going pink. "How do I pay you back for this?"

"You sit back and relax, sweetheart. Your happiness is all I want."

"You're so sappy."

"I never said I wasn't."

He chuckles, then leans back into the padded seat with a sigh, stretching out his long legs. "This is *so* much better than Economy."

I lean around the edge of my own seat —I've chosen the aisle so Ro can feel more privacy between me and the window— and peer down the aisle, watching as people grumble and grizzle their way into the tighter quarters in Economy behind us. There, they are sitting three abreast against the windows and in rows of four down the center of the plane. They look squished together. I cringe and turn back to look at Rowan, imagining how he must have felt, stressing about his condition in such cramped conditions.

I don't say anything about that, though. I just grab for his hand, then bring it to my lips, grazing his knuckles with a kiss as light as air. "I'm happy to give this to you, baby."

Before we boarded, we visited the bathrooms, and when I changed our seats with the airline, I requested a row closer to the onboard Business Class toilets, too. We're only two rows away from the currently green-lit door, and I hope that also gives Rowan some additional comfort. There are fewer people to fend off in our section of the plane, and I have spare pullups for him in case he still can't make it in time. They'll be easy enough to stash discretely into the inside pocket of his jacket if he needs them. And, if I get my way and he sleeps through some of the flight, he *will* need them.

After takeoff, we spend a little time ignoring our in-flight entertainment screens in favor of looking through some of our photos and talking about our favorite parts of the past week. I also show him some of the sights I saw before I got to the Sunshine Coast, watching his smile turn wistful.

"We should consider coming back in a year or two," I say as his eyes take in the selfie I took outside of the Sydney Opera House. "I could show you some of the places I went, and maybe we could go to some places that are new to both of us."

His eyes are wide as he looks up from his phone screen and at my face. "That's...some serious future planning."

My heart squeezes but I smile reassuringly. "I'm a planner, sweetheart. It's part of my job as Daddy."

I half expect him to argue or brush me off, but his smile turns bashful and he nods. "You're good at that," he murmurs, leaning in. "At being Daddy. If...if I haven't made it clear...I love it." He clears his throat and nibbles his lip, then murmurs, "I...I love you, actually."

We would so get caught if I dragged him into the bathroom to join the Mile High Club.

Unable to do that, because being arrested for public indecency or whatever consequence being caught fucking in an airplane bathroom gets you isn't on my To Do list, I groan and wrap my hand around the back of his head, pulling him in for a searing kiss. I get hard, from the echoing words in my head and the delicious sensation of our tongues entwining, and I don't stop. Not until I need to breathe.

Then I pull back and rest my forehead against his, replying, "I love you, too, Ro."

Yes, it has only been a week, but how could I not fall head-over-heels in love with this man? He's so sweet, and kind, and we're so compatible. This week together has opened up a world of opportunity, and opened my eyes to just how very incompatible Jerry and I were. He was right to end things, and I have never been more grateful that he did.

Chapter Fifteen

"So," Bianca drops into the chair across from my large desk, leaning back and crossing her ankles on the polished surface, the soles of her black heels facing me, "you look well rested."

She marched into my office, all dark hair and attitude in her power suit, telling me that it was my lunch break and that we were eating in. That was three minutes ago, and after sweet talking my assistant into shuffling a couple of my afternoon meetings, I finally sat back down in my chair to face my best friend.

Over the week I spent in Australia, I replied to her texts sporadically. I sent her photos and vague updates about my activities, but I didn't indulge the long deep and meaningful conversations that we usually share. I should have assumed that Bianca would come looking for me as soon as she knew I was back and active.

I smile at her, feeling exactly as she's said. Rested. Happy. Relaxed.

Grateful.

"I am," I nod, then reach for the paper bag she dropped on my desk, pulling out the chicken sandwiches and fries she bought from the café downstairs. I slide hers across to her and dive into mine with gusto. I sigh happily after my first bite. "Thank you."

The words hold more weight than a simple thanks for lunch, and I know she hears it.

Sweeping her feet back off my desk, she scoots her chair forward and eyes me seriously. "You really did enjoy it?"

"I did. Way more than I thought I would. It was…" I pause, searching for the words to explain just how much her generous gift has changed my life. Choked up, and not just because I've taken another bite of my sandwich, I swallow and finish tearfully, "perfect, Bee."

Her green eyes widen almost comically. "Rowan," my name comes out on a wave on concern, "are you…Jesus, babe, are you *crying?*"

Letting out a decidedly watery chuckle, I shrug and wipe at my eyes. "I, um," I try to clear my throat while I blink rapidly. "I met someone." If her eyes get any wider, I'm afraid they might fall out of their sockets. "And, um, I know it's fast, and it sounds crazy, but I love him."

"*Whoa,*" she breathes, awed. Then her brow crinkles and she leans forward. "Is he Australian? Oh, babe, is he still over there while you're here?"

I shake my head, trying to get my emotions under control. "No," I laugh again, sounding mildly manic even to my own ears. "Get this: he lives *here*. Like *here* here. Half an hour from my apartment."

"*What?!*"

"I know, right? What are the chances?"

"I'm gonna need the whole story."

So, I spend the next few minutes giving her the summarized —and abridged to avoid all mention of my *issues* or our kinkier play— story. Bianca tuts and shakes her head through parts of it, scowling and muttering about the booking fiasco under her breath, and asks questions about Aaron which stall the process. But she's smiling as I wrap the whole thing up, looking about as bewildered as I've felt since I met him.

"If I believed in fate…" she muses, biting into her sandwich again.

I swallow my own mouthful and nod. "I'm starting to think that maybe I should. The way everything had to line up *just right* for us to meet…it feels like I'm living in my very own romcom."

"You hate romcoms," she accuses, making me laugh.

"I'm coming around to them."

Sitting back in her seat, Bianca's gaze turns assessing again. Her lips quirk into the ghost of a smirk and she says, "I want to meet this guy."

"We've only been together for, like, a week and two days."

"Uh-huh," she waves a dismissive hand, "and you've already said you love him. *And* he's changed your feelings on romcoms. I can't *not* meet him."

If our roles were reversed, I would be making the same demand of her. I sigh. "Yeah, well, I haven't seen him since we left the airport the other day." It was hard to walk away from him, even harder to get into my car and drive myself back home, but the barrage of texts and phone calls we have exchanged since then has soothed the ache in my chest a little. "So, you know, give me a little while longer to enjoy him for myself first. Please?"

Understanding softens her expression before she nods. "Of course, babe. But I'm still giving him the shovel talk."

"I wouldn't expect anything less."

***

I'm nervous as I park my car in the visitors' lot of the nondescript apartment building downtown. It's not the kind of place I imagined Aaron would live. Not when I know how vibrant he is. But then, he did say he prefers to spend his money on experiences rather than material things, so that probably includes his apartment, too. Especially when he doesn't get to spend a lot of time at home, thanks to his busy work schedule.

The building looks just like every other one in this area: tall, rectangular, built out of gray concrete and brick. But the lobby is light and airy, though minimalist, and I travel to the tenth floor in a clean, brightly lit elevator. There, I turn to the right and make my way down the hall.

There are two apartments on every floor, and Aaron lives in the one with the view of the college and its sprawling grounds. The other side of the building faces the more industrial part of the city. I smile to myself, thinking that it makes sense he would prefer to see splashes of parkland and greenery in his view. That's very much like my Daddy.

Adjusting the strap of my overnight bag on my shoulder, I rap my knuckles on the door and try not to fidget as I wait. It has been almost a week since I last saw him, and I can't help but worry that, despite our constant contact over the phone and via text, he might have changed his mind about being with me.

But those concerns fade away as the door swings open and I'm met with his blinding smile.

"Hey, baby," he greets me, reaching forward to tug me inside. I barely register the sound of the door closing and the lock engaging as I'm enveloped in his warmth and scent. "God, I've missed you."

Melting into his embrace, I fight the ridiculous urge to cry. "I've missed you, too, Daddy."

He groans and kisses my cheek, murmuring, "You know exactly which buttons to press, don't you, honey?" There's a teasing glint in his eyes as he pulls back to look at me, but something of my emotional state must show on my face because it is immediately replaced with concern. "Oh, Ro. Sweetheart, c'mere."

I don't know why I'm fighting back tears as I'm pulled into another strong hug, but Aaron knows exactly what to do. He slips my bag from my shoulder and drops it by the door, then leads me into the open-plan living area of his apartment, pulling me into his lap as he drops onto the couch.

He rubs my back and soothes me as I sniffle in his hold, rubbing a stubbly, spiky cheek over my temple. "It's been a long week, huh?" his voice rumbles through his chest. "And after a week of being able to be completely free, it must have been hard for you to go back to masking everything."

I hadn't really thought about it that way.

But he's right.

From remembering to set alarms to visit the bathroom, to diapering myself at night, to not being able to give in to that floatier headspace where I'm coming to realize I do regress a bit, just like he said I do...it has been really draining. Emotionally and physically.

I find myself nodding and crying a bit harder.

"It's alright, baby. Let it out. Daddy's got you."

The magic words. They're apparently exactly what I needed to hear. After choking back one more sob, I stop trying to hold it all back. Burying my face into the crook of his neck, I cry it all out, finally letting the rush of relief wash over me as I stop pretending to be so controlled. So *adult.*

Aaron hums and sways us from side to side where we sit, his hand still rubbing circles on my back. I ride the whole emotional release out until I'm a snotty, sniffling, hiccupping mess. But I feel boneless and lighter than I have all week.

And *young*.

So young.

Even though I'm physically bigger than Aaron, right now I feel small, huddled in his lap. And...I like it. A lot. Why did I spend a week denying myself this indulgence?

"Feeling better now, sweetheart?" he asks.

My brain feels like mush. I can't really form words. "Mmm," I hum and nuzzle my face into him more.

After a beat, he asks, "Is talking hard right now?"

I nod, making another "Mmhmm" sound.

"Huh." His chest rises and falls quickly, and at the back of my brain, I register the light puff of air through my hair as a huff of dry amusement. "You feeling Little, baby?"

"Mmm," I nod again.

"And sleepy?"

My eyes *do* feel quite heavy. I'm drained, but the floatiness that I spent all week trying to fight off in Australia is more intense than ever. I force another nod. "Mmm."

"Okay," he brushes his lips over the top of my head, then jostles me before holding up a picture of a traffic light, illuminated on his phone screen. I squint at it, wanting to close my eyes and drift off, but Daddy has other ideas. "Because words are too difficult right now, I need you to point to your color, sweetheart."

Clumsily, I stab my index finger at the green circle.

"Good boy," Daddy praises softly, then adds, "and what's your color if I want to check your diaper and change you, honey?"

Another swat at the green circle, followed by a discontented whine when he makes me stand up. I was comfortable sitting in his lap!

Gently guiding me through his apartment, Daddy leads me into the nursery he told me about. I take it in drowsily, smiling at the gaming station he has set up on one side of the room —which I know he installed this week, because his ex was into stuffies and race cars and I'm not— and then the adult-sized changing table on the other side of the room, which is where he takes me.

There's a series of steps built against the side, so I can climb up easily. Once I'm settled on my back on the padded, plastic-covered surface, Daddy stands at the foot of the table, his hand splayed over my crotch.

Even through the thick denim, I'm sure he can feel the squish of the wet protection I'm wearing, but I don't feel even the slightest hint of embarrassment at having been caught in a wet diaper during the day. I'm still feeling that strange sense of detachment, where it actually feels kind of good to be in a diaper. To know that I can let go and that Daddy is looking after me. It cements that *smallness* in my head, but in a pleasant way.

"You're being so good for me right now, Ro," Daddy says, unbuttoning my jeans and lowering my zipper. "Can you lift your hips for me?"

I do as he says, then relax back as he launches into the routine I got so used to during our week at the resort. The further into it we get, the more light and floaty my head feels. I can't even focus on the adult thoughts about how this table is the perfect height for him to rut his cock against mine for more than a brief moment before my eyelids are drooping shut as the comforting weight of a dry, padded night-time diaper is closed over my crotch and taped snuggly against my hips.

"I'm not big and strong enough to carry you to bed, sweetheart," Daddy laments, rousing me from my near nap, "so climb down carefully and walk with me, okay? We still need to get you into comfy jammies, too."

I *do* like the sound of comfy pajamas.

With limbs feeling like lead, I let him guide me down from the table and I waddle-walk into the bedroom across the hallway. It's a larger room, with a wide window looking out over the parkland and college grounds and the sprawling cityscape beyond, but I'm drawn to the plush-looking king-sized bed, and the even softer-looking blue pajamas emblazoned with sharks spread out on top of the comforter.

"Do you like them?" Daddy asks as I reach out to feel the soft fabric between my fingers. They're going to be warm, but not too thick and constrictive in the climate-controlled apartment.

I nod. "Mmm."

When I turn to face him, there's a soft, affectionate smile on his face. "Let's get you dressed, then."

I stand, loose and pliant, as he helps me out of my jeans, jacket and long-sleeved t-shirt. It's a lot more work than at the resort, because of the extra layers, but he doesn't seem to mind. Then, once I've climbed into the soft, long pajama pants and have the matching long-sleeved top buttoned, Daddy gestures for me to climb into bed, and then he joins me, spooning against my side with a satisfied sigh.

"I've missed this," he says, while I press my cheek to his chest, tucked in under his chin. Under my ear, I can hear his heart thumping away at a steady rhythm. My eyes finally slide shut while

I enjoy the ministrations of his fingers carding through my hair. "My sweet Boy," he coos. "Have a sleep, sweetheart. I'll still be here when you wake up. Then we can have a late dinner and talk."

For the first time in a week, I feel fully relaxed and so I drift off without any further encouragement.

Chapter Sixteen

Aaron

Once again, Rowan has surprised me. Cuddling him while he naps, I can't help thinking about his unexpected deep regression right now, to the point of being nonverbal. I know part of that comes from the shock to his system, having gone from a week of twenty-four-seven Daddy care to a week of forced adulting with only texts and phone calls to fill in the void our forced separation left. But it also shows how deeply he trusts me, and how comfortable he is getting with the idea of our dynamic as Daddy and Boy.

And what a dynamic it is turning out to be! He's unlike any other Little I've played with before. The juxtaposition of the diapers and now the nonverbal regression, coupled with his generally more adolescent headspace is going to keep me on my toes, but in the best ways imaginable.

I assume that, even with him being unable to muster words, he didn't regress into a toddler kind of headspace. He's already expressed his disinterest in other 'baby' play —no sippy cups, no stuffies, no blocks or cars or other 'younger' toys— and I doubt that will have changed just because he found it difficult to form words. Obviously, I won't know for sure until we can talk about it, and about how he feels about these new developments, but I've been around enough Littles in my time to have developed a sixth sense when it comes to the things they enjoy in headspace.

Fate really has dropped the perfect man for me right into my lap, hasn't it?

My phone buzzes in my pocket, and I smile when I fish it out, finding a text from Vince.

Vince:

Have fun with your Boy tonight, man.

And that was yet another surprise I discovered this week. Vince is also a Daddy, and his best friend, Anson, who works as a pediatrician in the same hospital as us, is a Little. I came across this discovery by complete accident, overhearing a conversation in the ED's staff change room. They were talking about visiting The Grove, a local kink club, and had no idea I had just stepped out of the shower. As soon as Vince teased Anson about behaving lest Anson's Daddy find out and punish him, I cleared my throat and made myself known, before telling them that I am also in the lifestyle.

Vince had snorted and shaken his head, muttering 'What are the chances?', while Anson's eyes lit up and he pestered me about my relationship status. That led to me unloading on them about the magical week spent on vacation, and about how much I missed Rowan already. It was such a relief to find people who understand, and by the end of our ten-minute conversation in the change room, I felt like I suddenly had two close friends in the city.

I tap out my reply to Vince's text, daring to imagine a time where Rowan might feel comfortable making friends with them, too. From what I have gathered from conversations over the past week, Anson is a little Little who enjoys ABDL play with his Daddy, and Vince's boyfriend, Bear, is a lifestyle Little who spends most of his time in a younger headspace, too. Perhaps finding friends like them might help Rowan to feel less lonely and self-conscious about his medical situation. Or, at least, it might be nice for him to see other Daddies and their Littles in action.

Me:

It's amazing seeing him again. I've missed him.

Vince:

LOL. That's an understatement. You've been a grumpy ass for the past few days, Park.

Me:

I have not.

Vince:

Grumpy for you, I mean. Still nicer than Dr Malone on a good day.

I chuckle to myself, thinking about our cantankerous colleague, who should have retired at least five years ago, and reply.

Me:

That's not exactly a difficult benchmark.

Vince:

All I'm saying is you probably should have tried to see him at least three days ago. I thought you were going to slap Benji with your clipboard today.

> Benji needs a proper paddling and we both know it.

The orderly in question is the walking, talking textbook definition of 'brat' if ever I saw one. Whether he's in the lifestyle or not makes no difference. And, okay, maybe I have been in a mood if my patience has run so thin that his usually humorous bratting got under my skin today.

> Is that what you would have told HR?

I chuckle again.

> Yep. They'd probably agree with me.

I think half the hospital would. Don't get me wrong, Benji is a nice guy, if a bit brazen. But he has a habit of rubbing people the wrong way sometimes.

> I'm just glad you didn't let your intrusive thoughts win and that you've got your Boy to make it all better.

> Bear and I hope we can meet him some day.

Smiling at how close to my own thoughts his are, I tap out one more reply before tossing my phone aside to focus on snuggling with my Boy.

> Me too.

***

"How are you feeling?" I ask as Rowan stirs to wakefulness a couple of hours later. He smiles sheepishly at me.

"Better. I...uh, I wasn't expecting to, um, meltdown like that. But...I needed it. And you were perfect, Daddy. Thank you."

I blink before grinning and swooping down for a kiss. I won't lie: I was prepared for him to be embarrassed or freaking out over regressing so deeply, and not for him to be so cool with it. Not that I'm not glad that he is.

"You're perfect," I tell him, not at all concerned by how sappy I sound. "I'm glad that helped. You're always safe to drop into whatever headspace you need with me, sweetheart."

Nodding, Rowan yawns, then says, "I didn't realize how much I've come to rely on having you around. Like...having to be in control of my own schedule again, bathroom breaks and changing myself...it's been draining."

"Speaking of," I reach for his crotch out of habit, but pause before I make contact. "Color?"

"Green. And I'm dry." He sighs and shrugs. "For now, anyway. But..." a coy smile stretches his lips. Any hint of his previous headspace is well and truly gone for now, "why don't we both get a bit wet?"

***

Minutes later, we step into the shower together. Like at the resort, the shower in my apartment is large enough to fit two adult men comfortably. It's a very plain, modernist bathroom, all white tiles and chrome accents, but it is comfortable and does exactly what I need it to.

I've set the water to warm, but not too hot. The pressure is perfect as it cascades over my skin and then, as I adjust the showerhead, over Rowan. I turn in his arms and smooth my hands over his shoulders, then the salt-and-pepper hair covering his pecks and abdomen. It feels so damn good to be reunited with him, to be kissing under the shower's spray while we get reacquainted so intimately.

Ro said he wanted to wash off the grittiness of his dried tears, and to clean himself properly after having been so thoroughly wet earlier. I didn't need to hear the justification: I won't ever turn down an opportunity to be naked and up close with him.

I'm half-hard already, but I'm not rushing through any of this. I'm letting Rowan set the pace, to see what he feels up to given his emotional catharsis.

We wind up pressed together under the steady spray of water, our lips and tongues sliding together while he slides a thigh between mine and presses me against the cool, tiled wall. I rut into his hip, moaning at how good it feels to have his larger body pressed so thoroughly against mine. He smiles against my lips.

"I have to pee, Daddy," he murmurs.

Leaning back, I try to gauge his sense of urgency as I ask, "Are you comfortable going here in the shower? Or would you rather use the potty?"

Rowan's smile turns coy, and he dips his chin. "Actually," he says, reaching down between us to grasp himself, "I've been doing some reading..."

Arching an eyebrow at him, my heart skips a beat at the third potential option.

He can't mean...

"What if..." he clears his throat, "what if I peed...on you?"

With blood rushing in my ears —which should be impossible, considering just how quickly my cock just sprang to full mast— I swallow roughly.

He's smirking a little now, pressing his dick into my belly, likely using the pressure to hold back if the urge to pee has suddenly hit him.

"Really?" my question is breathless.

We discussed my watersports kink a lot last week, but beyond that first unplanned session on the couch, we haven't explored it further. I assumed it would be something we would need to talk through properly, to plan for, but Rowan is full of surprises tonight and I am living for it.

He nods, rocking his hips into me while water continues to sluice over us. "I need to *go*, Daddy."

My eyes flutter shut as I groan, and his wicked chuckle feels like a reward.

"Will you let me mark my territory? Paint you as mine?"

"Jesus," I hiss, my balls drawing up with just how hot his dirty talk is.

"That's not my name, Daddy," he teases.

Opening my eyes, I search his gaze, finding nothing but heat and desire in them.

What the hell happened to my sweet, shy, embarrassed Boy?

"Wh-where is this coming from?" I ask him as I try to get myself under control. "Because it's fucking sexy, sweetheart, but...very new for you."

He nods, water-darkened hair falling over his forehead. "Like I said, I've done some reading this week. Uh, a *lot* of reading. About the kinky stuff." Now there's a blush creeping up his chest and towards his cheeks. "And I remembered...y'know...*the couch* and it...it sounded *really* good." He grinds his hips into me, gasping, "And I really do have to pee."

"Fuck," I breathe, "baby, that's so hot."

I don't know if I'm talking about the reading, his interest in trying new things, his sudden instigation of it, or just the confession that he's desperate to go. All of it, maybe.

"So...you want...?"

I drop to my knees in front of him, his cock at my eye level. He steps back a bit, bracing one hand on the tile above me and gripping his dick with the other.

"Oh, God," he almost whimpers, looking down at me with even more fire in his expression, "seeing you on your knees for me is...*nnnngh.*" The hand on his dick tightens its hold. "How..." he bites his lip. Uncertainty replaces some of the heat in his gaze. "Where do you want me to...?"

"Anywhere," I answer, stroking my own cock as I stare back up at him. "We're in the shower, sweetheart, and I have no limits with this." My gaze is pointed. "None, baby."

"Oh, fuck," his eyes close and his Adam's apple bobs. "D-Daddy..."

"You've been such a good boy holding on for me," I praise him, enjoying the way he shudders happily at the words. "So good for asking for what you want, too."

A whine escapes him, and his fingers tighten further around his cock. I wonder if it's painful.

I wonder if he likes that.

"I...I can't hold it, Daddy..."

"You can let go now, baby," I soothe, low and seductive. The water isn't making for great lube as my fist shuttles over my erection, but I couldn't care less. "Let Daddy see."

The second he loosens his grip, his bladder releases with an audible hiss. He aims at my chest, and the heat of it —even against the warmth of the shower water— is almost a shock at first. The feeling of his own internal body temperature coating me is almost euphoric.

"Open your eyes," I demand, "watch how well you're painting me up, Ro."

"Oh, *fuck*," he murmurs, looking down as the golden liquid drips down my chest, quickly rinsed away by the shower. With growing confidence, he steps closer as the gush becomes a dribble, still aiming for my skin, as if he wants to see me wear every drop.

The wonder in his expression, coupled with his panting breaths and the sensory aspect of the experience have me on the edge of release, but then he's dropping to his knees in front of me and reaching for my cock, batting my hand away to take me over the edge himself.

My bossy baby, I think with affection.

"Stand up, Daddy," he demands, living up to his new nickname in my head. "I want...I want you to mark me up, too. P-paint my face with your cum."

Oh, God.

I scramble to obey, leaning my weight against the tile while I look down the length of my body, furiously jerking myself now. A squirt of body wash hastily applied to my palm makes the motion slicker and faster, and I have to force my eyes open to watch his face, dripping from the shower, waiting so expectantly for my load.

"I'm close, baby," I warn him, and he scoots closer, tilting his chin up and puffing his gorgeous, broad chest out.

"Give it to me, Daddy."

That's all it takes. The desire and need in his eyes does me in.

"Oh, fuck, fuck, *fuuuuuuck*," I all but roar as my orgasm explodes from me, casting splashes of pearly white fluid over his cheeks, lips, chin and nose. There's even a splodge on his forehead.

My legs feel like jelly as I ride out the last few moments, dribbling onto my fist and the floor of the stall.

Rowan reaches for his face, running his palm through the mess I made, and then takes it to his own cock, stroking over his semi-erection with a satisfied little sigh. My own dick twitches at the sight, but my refractory period isn't that short.

"*Fuck*," he breathes, sounding awed as he glances down at his lap, and I think I can understand why. He's never made a secret of his disappointment or frustration with his ED.

"Baby, stand up," I urge, "let me suck you."

He doesn't need any further encouragement, releasing his hardening cock to allow me to help him to his feet, where we then switch positions and I kneel before him, taking him into my mouth greedily.

I can taste myself on his skin and I moan around him, licking and sucking with fervor. I'm spurred on by his whines and his groans, his fingers tangling in my wet hair.

"A-Aaron," he chokes out after a short while, "I'm going to come."

I suck harder, swirling my tongue around his length before I take him to the back of my throat and attempt to swallow around him.

"Oh, *shit shit shit*," he pants out, the fingers in my hair clenching and tugging, making my scalp sting deliciously, "Aaro—oh, fuck—*Daddy!*"

In my mouth, his cock hardens damn near to the point of steel before his pulsing release coats the back of my tongue and my throat in short spurts. There's not a ton of cum, so I swallow it down easily, continuing to suckle on his length as it shrinks away, becoming flaccid again.

He yelps, hypersensitive, and pulls away, leaning against the shower wall with a dazed, glazed look in his eyes.

I push to my feet with a grunt, asking, "You okay, baby?"

He turns his head, water still trickling over his face. He makes no move to brush it or the wet locks of his hair on his forehead away. "I think...I think you just sucked my brain right out of my dick."

I grin back at him. "Good."

So far, I would say that reconnecting has been a roaring success.

Chapter Seventeen

S omehow, things become easier after our first night together in Aaron's apartment. I find it easier to let go of any and all control —of my body, of my headspace, of clinging to adult responsibilities— when we're together. But it's not without its drawbacks.

I have a few more accidents during my workdays, forgetting that I don't have a Daddy just waiting to clean me up and take care of me. I also struggle with Aaron's shift work and with not being able to see him as often as I would like, because being without him makes me anxious, especially when I'm paranoid that my increased reliance on my protective underwear will at some point cause people to discover my condition.

But I am overall far too happy to allow these teething problems to create larger issues for both of us.

And when we are together, everything feels right.

On the nights when I'm alone at home, I research and read about the lifestyle I have fallen into. BDSM, age play, watersports...all these words that I once associated with porn have taken on completely different meanings. It's not just about getting down and dirty —though we do a lot of that, too— but about trust and support and, yeah, power dynamics, too. It makes me feel happy and empowered in ways I never imagined I could.

Like Aaron said when we first met, indulging in these kinks turns the tables on what I once believed was a flaw. Now, losing control of my bladder leads to much more positive experiences, whether they be sexy (like the watersports), or warm and affectionate (like the reverent diaper changes).

Now that I am more comfortable with it all, I'm even starting to consider Aaron's suggestion of meeting other people in the lifestyle. To feel like the way I'm living my life is normal. To feel like we can go out and be our authentic selves without judgement.

But it's a scary thought to let other people see our dynamic. Even if they are like us. Like me.

But Daddy was telling me about his friends who are in Daddy/Little relationships and I felt...not *jealous*, but...*something*. Like I want to be involved in their inside jokes and group chats, too. Not to keep tabs on my Daddy, but to feel included. And, on some level, I want to meet them for him. To show him that he isn't my dirty little secret. That I'm not ashamed of what we do together. He deserves to have balance in his life, too. We both do. As partners. Equals in our relationship.

"I wanna meet your friends," I blurt out, my thoughts tumbling past my non-existent filter. I'm in what he calls my Middle headspace, feeling young and impulsive and free. This headspace comes with very little tact, I've discovered.

Sitting beside me on the other beanbag in the nursery, Daddy sets down his Nintendo Switch controller and turns bodily to face me.

Secretly, I think he's just tired of having his ass whooped in Mario Kart.

"So, that came out of nowhere," he prompts, looking somewhere between amused and concerned. "Want to talk me through that thought process?"

I sigh and explain the rambling musings that got me to that point, adding, "It's not like I can always keep you to myself, right? And I trust that if I'm uncomfortable, we can cut things short. I just...I want to try. Not just for you, but for myself, as well."

He's quiet as he mulls it over. I can see the cogs turning behind those sharp, dark eyes of his. He doesn't question my conviction, though, and I appreciate that he trusts me enough to take me at my word.

"Would you prefer to start slowly? Maybe just meet Vince and Bear, or Anson and Drake? Or visit the Little Community Center to get some information?"

I like the idea of meeting his friends on neutral ground, but I appreciate that he's also considered the fact that I might want to ease into meeting them, too. But I am a grown man, and, despite my issues, I am used to meeting with new people every day. In many ways, meeting his friends should be easier, because I don't need to hide my condition from them. I don't need to worry about them thinking I'm disgusting or weird.

"Can we meet them at the Center?" I ask. "I don't think I'm ready for a BDSM club yet, but...a safe space where our lifestyle is...well, encouraged, I guess, sounds really nice."

A slow smile grows over his face, and he gives his head a little shake. "You'll never stop surprising me, will you sweetheart?"

"I've gotta keep you on your toes, Daddy. That's my job."

✳✳✳

The Little Community Center isn't far from my office building. I shouldn't have been surprised that Daddy managed to arrange for his friends to come at some short notice, but we agree to meet there for lunch on Sunday, after Vince's late shift finished.

Aaron and I arrive first, though, giving me time to get comfortable and meet some other people in the lifestyle before his friends get here. My nerves are jangled as we approach the large, sprawling building. It's one story and, from the sidewalk and much to my amusement, it looks like a large, modern daycare center. From the cream-colored stucco walls, to the rainbow sign and double doors, it is bright and inviting.

That feeling follows through once we walk through the front doors into a large, open-plan space with couches and tables and chairs, and a welcoming reception desk where a pretty woman with honey-blonde hair swept up into a ponytail sits. She smiles widely as we cross the big room, recognition dawning in her eyes as they land on Daddy.

"Hi, Aaron," she greets him warmly, "it's nice to see you again." She turns her attention to me. "Hi, I'm Cherie. Welcome to our center."

"Thanks," I reply, feeling a little awkward, but not as much as I'd anticipated, "I'm, uh, Rowan."

"Rowan," she repeats, as if memorizing my name. Her eyes flick between us again, then land on me, "What brings you in today? One of the Q and A sessions? A meeting with one of our counselors?" She gestures broadly towards the open room behind us, "Or to just chill out and make some new friends? I think I saw Spence and Tony setting up to play Candyland a little while ago."

"We're meeting some friends here, actually," Aaron answers easily. "The Littles will probably take advantage of your toys and games, though."

Cherie chuckles. "And the hot chocolate, too, I'm betting." She leans forward, conspiratorially, "Katie totally found herself having corner time for having one too many of those yesterday. She was practically bouncing off the walls."

Aaron snorts. "You've got your hands full with your Girl, Cher."

"I wouldn't have it any other way." Cherie turns to me and explains, "Katie is my wife. She's also a Little, and she thinks she's very cute when she's pushing boundaries."

I find myself smiling, relaxing into how easily she is talking about their relationship dynamics. It makes me feel confident enough to admit, "I'm more Middle than Little, I think. But I'm really new to this, and I'm still" —I pause, considering my phrasing— "exploring everything, I guess."

Her eyes light up and she claps her hands together. "That's wonderful to hear. Trying everything for the first time is kind of magical, in its own way." Her tone is wistful, but she shakes herself out of it and adds, "I'm glad you've come here. Charlie and Ash have really built something special for people in our community. You're safe here, Rowan. No question is too silly, no experience off-limits, as long as you're doing everything consensually and safely."

"Yeah, I've been looking on your website. This is all super impressive."

The founder, Charlie Walker, used to be a cop, according to the 'About Us' section online. A career-ending injury left him wanting to give back in other ways and, because he and his husband were in the BDSM lifestyle themselves, he thought having a kink-friendly space that wasn't a nightclub or sex club might help others. And I think it does. The center offers all sorts of services, from mentoring others in kink, to free counselling, to pro-bono legal advice, even access to beds and bathrooms for those who find themselves on the streets. It's all really commendable.

Cherie beams at me. "Charlie will be happy to hear that." She stands up and comes out from the office. "Let me give you the tour."

Cherie leads me and Aaron through the building, showing us where the bathrooms and changing rooms are, and I am unsurprised to find large stalls with oversized changing tables in them when I poke my head inside. Next, we see the two meeting rooms which, she explains, are used for Q and A sessions, support group meetings, and which can also be hired out for similar events. As we travel down the hallway, she points out the offices belonging to the legal team and counselling teams, and then takes us out back to a large sunroom spanning the length of the building. It is littered with toys of all kinds —stuffies, balls, ropes, large bells— and Cherie giggles at my perplexed expression as she stoops to pick up the toys and drop them into their corresponding tubs along the wall.

"This space is predominantly used for pet play," she explains, lobbing a tennis ball into a bucket of other balls. "We mostly see pups and kittens here, to be fair, but one of our regulars is a pony player. They enjoy trotting the length of the room and jumping over hurdles." A wave of her hand directs my gaze to a neatly stacked pile of plastic and foam shapes. "A lot of the pups like playing with those obstacles, too."

"Wow," I murmur, taking it all in. The idea of dressing and acting like an animal for fun and relaxation makes me feel like my regression —even with the diapers and watersports— is vanilla in comparison. "It's so cool that you have the space for them to play like that here."

"It is," she nods. "Some of the Littles love rolling around out here, too. Especially if they find a friendly pup to play with."

I can't quite imagine myself treating another adult like a pet, but I can see how others might find it fun. "Wow." I repeat.

"There's also a jungle gym and a swing set out back, but it's too cold and wet right now to go out there," she continues. "In summer, though, we've started hosting Littles days out there. We fire up the grill, get a sprinkler going...it's a blast."

I squirm on the spot, recalling how uncomfortable I was in my swim trunks at the resort. It was one thing to be able to hide my accidents in a pool or the ocean, but I don't think I'd be able to with just a sprinkler for cover. But then, here I could probably wear my incontinence pants without fear of feeling different. At least, not around a bunch of Littles.

Oblivious to my thoughts, Cherie shrugs. "Anyway," she says, "that's the tour. Before you leave today, I'll get you a welcome pack with contact numbers and flyers with our schedule of information sessions and support groups. You don't have to do anything with them, but I like to make sure everyone gets them."

"We'd love that," Aaron answers for me, obviously sensing the fact that I'm mildly overwhelmed. "But we might go make ourselves a couple of those hot chocolates and just cuddle while we wait for our friends, if that's okay."

Cherie ushers us back into the large lounge-type room cheerfully, showing us to the bench where there are paper cups and an assortment of coffee, tea, and cocoa sachets, along with a hot water dispenser and a fridge full of creamer and milk.

Daddy ushers me down onto a comfy, bright orange couch and makes our drinks for us, warning me that mine might be a bit hot and to sip carefully. I smile at his caution and care as I do as I'm told, letting the warm, sweet liquid warm me up from the inside.

"Good?" he asks, and I don't think he's only asking about the drink.

I nod. "Mmmhmm."

"It's a lot to take in, sweetheart," he says. "If you want to go home—"

"No," I shake my head, forcing myself to form words. Now isn't the time to drop into a nonverbal state. I can do that once we are home, when I will be comfortable enough let go completely. Maybe one day, I will be able to do so in public, but not yet. "No. I...I'm okay. Just...processing."

"Just safeword out if you need to, baby. The guys will understand."

I nod, already feeling more adult again. "I know, and I will if it gets to be too much."

Aaron kisses my cheek and rubs his nose along the skin above my beard. "Good boy. I love you."

Any remaining anxiety melts away. "I love you, too."

Chapter Eighteen

Aaron

Rowan seems to hit it off with Bear and Anson almost instantly. Even though both guys are significantly younger —especially Bear, who is only in his early twenties— they bond over some of their similarities as Littles.

Bear, who is petite, with a pretty, freckled face framed by a cloud of red, curly hair, is almost perpetually in a Little-to-Middle headspace. He encourages Ro to join him in a game of Uno, and Ro settles into it as soon as Bear starts openly calling Vince 'Daddy'. Then there's blonde and buff Anson, whose Little space is younger than either of the others, who is quite happy to turn in his seat and tell Drake he needs a diaper change.

"I peed," he says shamelessly, scrunching his nose. "I is *wet*, Daddy. Help. I feel yucky."

Ro blinks, watching wide-eyed as Drake shoulders the backpack they came in with and leads him by the hand to the change rooms. Nobody else bats an eye. In fact, Vince even takes the opportunity to ask Bear if he needs a potty break, though Bear shakes his head and says no.

I think we're all aware that Anson was making a point, normalizing the entire exchange for Rowan's benefit, but it doesn't make Ro any less awed to see it.

He wriggles in his own seat, then looks at me and whispers, "I'm wet, too, Daddy."

My heart almost bursts with how proud I am of him for being so brave. For not only trusting me, but for trusting my friends as well.

I tell him as much as I change him into a new pullup, and I also ask him if he is proud of himself, too. Because that's more important to me. I want him to make choices that make *him* happy. I will be happy regardless.

"I am," he says quietly, his cheeks flushed red. "It...it feels...I guess it's nice not to hide it. To...to feel normal." His voice breaks a little, and his lashes flutter madly. Tilting his head back, he huffs wetly. "God. These are happy tears, Daddy, I swear."

"It's okay to be overwhelmed though, honey," I cuddle him close. "You've tried a *lot* of new things today. It's confronting and scary."

"Your friends aren't scary," he laughs, brushing away the last of his emotional tears with the back of his hand. "I like them."

"We like you, too!" Anson's voice —sounding significantly more mature than he did a few minutes ago— sails over to us from the next stall, followed by Drake's deep groan and a chagrined, "Sorry!" before the sounds of him reminding his boy that eavesdropping is naughty travel over to us.

Rowan chuckles and leans into me again. "I really like them."

I grin. "I do, too."

***

Ro falls asleep on the drive back to my apartment. It's been a big day for him, and I imagine it has been emotionally and mentally draining, even if he did seem to enjoy himself. When we left, he was happy to agree to a playdate with Anson and Bear, and it didn't feel like he was only doing it for my sake.

As I had hoped, his spirits seemed lifted as he hung out with my friends. If I had to guess, not having to worry about the stigma of his condition —or of our dynamic— took a weight off his shoulders. Plus making friends with people with whom he can be completely authentic and not on his guard must feel good, too. I know it has felt good for me, having people in my circle who not only know that I'm a Daddy, but who *get it*.

A few months ago, when Jerry broke up with me and I uprooted my entire life, I worried that I would be isolated in a new city. That it would take time to find my footing and a new circle of kinky friends, let alone a Boy willing to indulge my watersports kink. The fact that it has all just kind of fallen into my lap without effort feels like a sign from the universe at this point. Like it was meant to be.

I know that my relationship with Rowan is still in its infancy. I know that we will have to work hard to find and maintain a proper balance, and that there will be times where we argue, or where we seemingly go backwards.

But right now, as he snores softly with his forehead against the cool glass of the passenger seat window in my car, my heart is full, and the future looks bright.

Epilogue

Rowan

"Summertime is the best!" Anson declares, stripping off his shirt to reveal a gym-chiseled abdomen which makes me a little self-conscious about my soft, middle-aged paunch.

He races through his and Drake's backyard and launches himself into the large, inflatable pool they have set up against the back fence. Drake sighs at the splash and shakes his head. "Leave some water in the pool for the others, sunshine."

"I'm not going in," I inform him, making a show of getting comfortable on the sunlounge I nabbed when Daddy and I arrived. It's facing the yard, and I am content to watch the other Littles cavort. "And I don't think Bear will mind if it's only half-full."

Bear is so sweet and easy-going, nothing seems to upset him. He makes fun wherever he goes, and I get a kick out of the way his mind works.

"Ash might want to sit in more than just a puddle, though," Daddy says, reminding me that Asher and Charlie will also be coming to this get-together, because Ash and Anson are good friends. It makes me a little nervous, because I don't really know the founders of The Little Community Center that well, but the work they do speaks for the kind of people they are.

I nod. "Fair."

Drake sighs. "I'll fill the pool some more."

From where he has been making a concerted effort to empty it with his splashing about, Anson cheers loudly. My lips twitch into a smile. He's definitely a character.

"Do you need a potty break, baby?" Daddy asks. Even though I'm not going in the pool, I'm not wearing my usual pullup under my shorts, and he knows I'm paranoid about my condition causing me issues, even though nobody here today would bat an eye if I wet my pants.

"Yes, Daddy," I tell him, realizing it has been a while since I last went. I don't want to tempt fate. He helps me out of my seat, and I try not to groan like an old man as I push to my feet, then he leads me through the ranch-style home to the bathroom.

Recently, part of our Daddy/Boy roleplay has included him 'helping' me in the bathroom, shuffling up behind me and placing his hands over mine as I aim into the toilet bowl. I can feel his cock twitch against my ass as the stream of liquid hitting water reaches my ears.

"Good boy," he croons lowly into my ear as he helps me shake, dab with paper, then tuck myself away.

I shiver at the heat in his tone.

"We're not being naughty here, Daddy," I tell him, wanting to be firm but sounding rueful even to my own ears.

"Pity," he sighs, then makes a show of adjusting himself before washing his hands at the basin with me. "You look so sexy in swim trunks. It makes me think of the resort."

Nibbling my lip, my stomach flutters at the reminder of how we met six months ago. I feel like a different person to the sad, lonely guy he rescued at that reception desk. I feel liberated now, much less self-conscious about my incontinence or my erectile dysfunction — not that I'm open about either issue with anyone outside of the new friends I have made in the kink community, mind you. But the thought of other people finding out about my incontinence no longer terrifies me quite as much. Not when I know now that it doesn't make me less desirable or lovable.

"We should go back," I tell him, mostly to distract myself from dropping to my knees even though I just said no naughty business, "to Australia, I mean. Like we talked about."

Daddy's eyes are knowing, and he sounds amused as we walk back towards the gathering out back, "Yeah?" he asks. "I thought you hated beaches and heat?"

There were a lot of things I thought I hated, myself and my issues included. But I'm not the same Rowan that got on that first plane to Brisbane. I'm different. Reset. Renewed, even.

Shooting Daddy a cheeky wink, I shrug, "Turns out, I just needed a Daddy to teach me how to enjoy myself properly."

"Is that so?" he laughs, then wraps his arm around me, spinning me so we are face-to-face and pressed against each other.

I nod, "Yup."

There's a world of subtext in his eyes when he tilts his head back, brushing his lips over mine, declaring, "Then, I guess it's a good thing you found one."

His lips are on mine, soft and sweet and loving, preventing any answer I might have come up with.

But he's right. It is a good thing that I found him, and I hope to keep him forever.

I guess this means I need to come up with a pretty birthday present for Bianca now.

I kind of owe her one.

THE END

Thank you so much for reading *Rowan's Renewal*. This is Book 2 in my *Kinks & Conundrums* series, which is prefaced by Book 0.5, *Baron's Boo-boo*, and Book 1, *Anson's Awakening*.

If you enjoyed this sweet, fluffy age play novella, which also functions as a spin off from my *Littles & Lace* series, you may also enjoy *Charlie's Contentment* — a 10,000 word novella set in the original *Littles & Lace* series. Currently, you can read *Charlie's Contentment* for free by signing up to my newsletter at:

https://annasparrows.com/newsletter-subscription/

Also, if you would consider leaving a rating or a review for *Rowan's Renewal*, I would be greatly appreciative. Ratings and reviews tell the algorithms which books to share, but they also help me continue to hone my skills as an author.

Thanks again for reading!

Love,

Anna

About the Author

I am a bi Aussie author living in Brisbane, Australia. I've been writing* for as long as I can remember. I started with silly short stories as a kid, moved on to fanfiction in my teens, and then to publishing original fiction in my thirties.

I have been an avid reader of MM romance my whole life. (Ask me about my beginnings with *Buffy* fanfic, haha!) I wrote a sweet and kinky MM romance novel in 2022 and the reader response changed my life. From there, I knew I had found my niche.

And thus Anna Sparrows was born.

*All of my writing is 100% my own. No part of it is generated by Artificial Intelligence (AI) software of any kind. Yes, that means that it's sometimes flawed, but I'm okay with that.

Follow Me

Website: https://annasparrows.com

Facebook: https://www.facebook.com/AnnaSparrowsAuthor

Instagram: https://www.instagram.com/annasparrows

Newsletter: https://annasparrows.com/newsletter-subscription

I write ridiculously sweet & steamy MM romance with guaranteed HEAs...and sometimes with a side of kink. My backlist can be found at annasparrows.com

Dads & Adages Series

Visit Australia's sunny Gold Coast where an assortment of single dads find love and even learn a few life lessons along the way.

Book 1: Where There's A Will

Book 2: You Don't Know Jack

Book 3: A Match Made In Evan

Book 4: Speak Of The Neville (release TBA)

Related: A Surprise For The Holidays

Written in 3rd person POV, *A Surprise for the Holidays* is a sweet, fluffy MM Christmas novella with a grumpy former soccer player turned coach, a golden retriever younger player, and a precocious little girl. Featuring an Aussie Christmas, grumpy/sunshine vibes, an age gap and sand where you're used to snow, this novella brings additional heat to the festive season in more ways than one!

Down Under Daddies Series

Set in rural Western Australia, come meet the and the kinkiest and queerest band of stationhands any outback cattle station has ever seen.

Book 1: A Stable Daddy

Littles & Lace Series

The Littles & Lace series is an MM Age Play series, following a group of like-minded friends in the BDSM community. You'll find mild ABDL, light Pet Play, Femme Play and more here.

Book 1: Asher's Answer

Book 2: Matteo's Mettle

Book 3: Ted's Temerity

Book 4: Spencer's Satisfaction

Book 5: Chance's Choice

Book 6: Josh's Jackpot

Shifters Sanctuary Series

In a world where alphas are thought to be extinct, a number of men are about to have their worlds rocked.

Book 1: His Alpha Unlocked

Book 2: His Prodigal Alpha

Book 3: His Unicorn Alpha

Book 4: His Dragon Duo (TBA)

Kinks & Conundrums Series

A spin-off from the Littles & Lace series, this series follows Daddies, Doms, Littles, and Pet Players as they discover their kinks and find love.

Book 0.5: Baron's Boo-Boo

Book 1: Anson's Awakening

Book 2: Rowan's Renewal

Co-Written With MJ Booth

Completely Pucked (an MM hockey age play romance)